Maxwell re
closer to him
responded, m

Maxwell touched a finger to her chin. His eyes were bright with an emotion she could identify.

Lust.

His mouth curved up at the corners. His finger brushed against her skin, moving back and forth, making it difficult for her to think.

Desire ignited in her belly, causing her to pull away reluctantly. She didn't want Maxwell to think that she was easy.

"What's wrong, sweetheart?"

"Nothing. I just don't think it's a good idea for us to get carried away," she murmured against his cheek.

Their gazes locked and both of them could see the attraction mirrored in the other's eyes.

Maxwell pulled her back into his arms.

Camille drew his face to hers in a renewed embrace. He kissed her again, lingering, savoring every moment. Camille's emotions whirled. Blood pounded in her brain, leaped from her heart and made her knees tremble.

"I have always been drawn to you, sweetheart," Maxwell said. "From the moment I laid eyes on you."

Books by Jacquelin Thomas

Kimani Romance

The Pastor's Woman
Chocolate Goodies
Teach Me Tonight
You and I
Case of Desire

JACQUELIN THOMAS

is an award-winning, bestselling author with more than
thirty-five books in print. When she is not writing, she
is busy working toward a degree in psychology. Jacquelin
and her family live in North Carolina.

JACQUELIN THOMAS

CASE OF DESIRE

KIMANI
ROMANCE

Bernard, you are my best friend and the love of my life.
There are no words to adequately express how honored
I am to be your wife. Thank you for being my #1 fan
and supporter. Other men should follow your example
as a husband, father and friend.

Special thanks and acknowledgment to Jacquelin Thomas
for her contribution to the Hopewell General miniseries.

KIMANI PRESS™

ISBN-13: 978-0-373-86232-0

CASE OF DESIRE

www.kimanipress.com

Printed in U.S.A.

Dear Reader,

When people work closely together in a high-emotion environment like a hospital—sharing highs, lows, victories and losses—a unique bond forms, often bringing two people together as friends, lovers or both. I really enjoyed writing *Case of Desire* because of my excitement over the entire Hopewell General series. It is always a pleasure to be partnered with such wonderful authors as Brenda Jackson, Maureen Smith and Ann Christopher.

Public relations director Camille Hunter and Maxwell Wade, the hotshot attorney from New York retained to fight an unlawful-termination lawsuit, find themselves falling in love as they work together to protect the teaching hospital's reputation. I hope you will enjoy getting to know them as you witness the birth of a love like no other.

As always, thanks for your support and please keep in touch. You can reach me at jacquelinthomas@yahoo.com.

Sincerely,

Jacquelin

Chapter 1

Alexandria, Virginia, the hometown of George Washington and Civil War General Robert E. Lee, attracted visitors from near and far, but Maxwell Wade wasn't in the city to take in glimpses of Alexandria's proud history. The last time he visited Alexandria, Maxwell had spent a day on the bustling waterfront on board a lunch and dinner cruise, and had visited several of the historic museums that preserved the city's important heritage.

This time Maxwell was in town on business. He had been retained to represent Hopewell General, one of the largest teaching hospitals in the country, in a wrongful termination lawsuit.

He pulled up to a stoplight and waited patiently for the light to change from red to green.

Maxwell felt the tiny hairs on the back of his neck stand up. He glanced out the window, his eyes landing on the gorgeous woman sitting in the car next to him. Maxwell smiled and gave a slight nod.

She batted her long lashes and returned his smile.

The light changed and Maxwell was on his way. He harbored no regret at not getting her name and number. He was not lacking when it came to women.

Maxwell pulled into a parking space ten minutes later. He got out of the car, grabbed his briefcase and strolled confidently across the lot and into the lobby of Hopewell General.

"Here comes the East Coast equivalent of the late, great Johnnie Cochran," a man announced as Maxwell approached the north elevator. "Congratulations on winning the Benson case."

"Thanks," Maxwell responded with a grin. "Ray, I hear your checkbook's a little lighter after Judge Hanson fined you for suggesting that she recuse herself from your case." He eyed his friend from law school for a moment, and then shook his head. "I heard that she is not one to mess with."

Ray Graham shrugged. "Hanson really needs to put in for her retirement. I'm pretty sure that she went to college with Moses."

Laughing, the two men stepped into the elevator when the doors opened. They rode up to the second floor, which housed the hospital's legal department.

"Max, I really appreciate you helping us out with the Matthews lawsuit," Ray said, leading Maxwell into his office. Dr. Terrence Matthews had been fired when it was discovered that he had a drug problem and now he was suing the hospital for wrongful termination.

"I'm glad you called. I understand that his family was the hospital's largest benefactor."

Ray nodded. "We have our annual fundraiser coming

up this month. Maxwell, we really need to settle this lawsuit before then. The hospital needs funding for our new cancer research center. Rupert and Sarah Matthews are no longer donors and we could lose others because of their influence."

Maxwell nodded in understanding. He followed Ray through a door leading into the legal offices.

Ray paused by his assistant's desk and said, "Angie, this is…"

"Oh, I am very familiar with Maxwell Wade," she quickly interjected. "Mr. Wade is the attorney who strikes fear in the hearts of all who oppose him."

Maxwell smiled warmly. "It's very nice to meet you, Angie."

"The pleasure is all mine," she responded, eyeing him hungrily.

He recognized the lustful gleam in her eye. At thirty-five years old, Maxwell had grown used to getting this type of reaction from women and it amused him.

Maxwell followed Ray into his office, closing the door behind him. They sat down to discuss more details of the Matthews lawsuit.

"I want to touch base with Camille Hunter at some point today," he told Ray. "We exchanged a few emails, but I want to speak with her in person."

"She's worked hard to keep this lawsuit from being the focus of the hospital," Ray stated. "The Matthews family, on the other hand, is doing everything in their power to discredit Hopewell General. They are in denial about Terrence's drug problem."

"They are claiming that he was set up," Maxwell commented.

"Yes," Ray confirmed.

Maxwell scanned through the documents of the case.

"Well, we will just have to prove that Terrence abuses drugs. I will bet that his parents have him stashed away somewhere in rehab right now. If we can find out where, maybe we can get this resolved quickly." Maxwell was used to winning at everything he did, from the boardroom to the bedroom.

He loved his hard-charging, hard-playing life and wouldn't change a thing. He found it incomprehensible that his good buddy Thomas Bradshaw recently married and was already a father. He had stunned Maxwell with the news that he had eloped with the mother of his son.

Ray made a couple of phone calls while Maxwell continued to read through the statements and documents of the lawsuit, jotting down notes here and there.

Maxwell pulled out his iPhone and sent a quick email to Camille Hunter, requesting a time to meet. He was looking forward to meeting the head of public relations for the hospital.

Camille Hunter pulled the folds of her coat together to ward off the winter chill as she walked briskly through the hospital doors. She loved her job as the director of public relations at the prestigious Hopewell General Hospital. At twenty-five years old, she had worked at the hospital for six years, beginning when she was a college student.

The moment she walked through the lobby doors of the hospital, Camille could feel a buzz of excitement in the air and it had nothing to do with the upcoming Christmas season.

She walked over to where a small group of interns were huddled and asked, "Hey, what's going on?"

"I just met Maxwell Wade," one of them responded.

"Oh, my goodness, that man is gorgeous. I've never seen anyone look that good."

Camille laughed. "Isabelle, you make it sound as if he's the only handsome man in the world." She secretly believed that Isabelle Morales, a Jennifer Lopez look-alike, was on the hunt for a rich man to marry.

"He's well over six feet tall and very muscular. You know how much I love tall men, and that suit he was wearing this morning looks like it was made just for him."

"It probably was," one of the other women interjected. "He can certainly afford to have a personal tailor on his payroll."

"I just love his long lashes," another cooed.

"Wait until you see him, then you'll know what I'm talking about," Isabelle told Camille. "That Maxwell Wade looks better in real life than in his pictures."

A couple of the other interns nodded in agreement.

"He is absolutely yummy," Isabelle stated. "I don't know how I'm going to get my work done with that sexy piece of chocolate in this hospital."

"Then maybe it's best that I don't meet him," Camille joked. "With all of the stuff piled on my desk, I need to be able to focus on my work."

"I heard he's currently single," one of the other interns interjected. "He and that model Kendra Dixon broke up a few months ago."

"Is she the one with the reality show?" Camille asked. She recalled reading something about it in *People* magazine while getting a pedicure.

Isabelle played with a curling tendril. "Yeah, she's the one. As for Maxwell Wade, he won't be alone for much longer if I have anything to do with it."

Camille chuckled as she shook her head. "Isabelle, I don't know about you."

"Hey, I have no problem going after what I want."

"We know," two of the other interns said in unison.

Camille laughed. "I'll see you girls later."

She stopped to talk with one of the pediatric physicians before heading to her office. The hospital was buzzing about the handsome multimillionaire Maxwell Wade. Camille had yet to meet the man in person, but she had read enough articles about him.

She and Maxwell had been exchanging emails for the past couple of weeks and his aggressive, confrontational style had rubbed her the wrong way from their first email exchange. He was a very handsome man, but she was not about to join the scores of women falling on their faces to worship him.

Humming softly, Camille sat down at her desk. The first thing on her agenda was to check her email. She was expecting an email with the menus for the annual holiday charity ball. Hopewell General's charity ball was the grande dame of fundraising parties—a formal, black-tie dinner and dance dating back to the 1950s when the hospital was established.

Theme and décor had always been important elements of the fundraising event. Poinsettias and Japanese lanterns created the ambience for the first one, so Camille decided to recreate that very first charity ball by using ultra-modern silver and black décor with dramatic lighting. Entertainment for that night would include a series of living portraits telling the history of the hospital.

Along with dinner, dancing and great entertainment, Camille had planned a silent auction with some fantastic prizes, which included fishing charters, hotel and resort spa getaways, and gift cards to local merchants.

She heard Dr. Germaine Dudley's voice in the hallway and froze.

"Please don't let him come in here," she whispered. "My morning started off great and I don't want it ruined."

Camille had been avoiding Hopewell's chief of staff since he made some comments to her a couple of days ago that made her uncomfortable. It was possible that she had misunderstood what he'd meant, but for now, she just hoped to remain out of his path.

"What's up, girl?"

She looked up from her monitor to find Jerome Stubbs standing in her doorway. Jerome was her best friend and an O.R. nurse. She smiled at him and asked, "How was your date last night with Julie?"

He grinned. "We never made it to dinner. Julie's a wild woman."

Camille held up a hand. "Enough said."

Jerome checked his watch, and then strolled into the office carrying a cup of his favorite coffee. He sat down in one of the visitor chairs facing Camille. "You mean you don't want to hear about my night of passion?"

She laughed. "No, I really don't."

"Don't want to get all hot and bothered, huh?" he teased.

"Jerome, don't you have to be somewhere?" Camille asked.

He shook his head. "Nope. I came in early just so that I could spend some time with my best friend." Jerome took a long sip of his delicious-smelling coffee. "I heard that Maxwell Wade is here in the hospital."

Camille leaned back in her chair. "Why on earth is this big news? Jerome, I just don't get it."

Jerome laughed. "I hear you, but you know how it is. He's world renowned and he's handled some of the top high-profile cases in the country. Maxwell Wade is a celebrity to these people."

"He's a lawyer. One who was hired to help us with this mess that Terrence created." Camille released a soft sigh. "I never thought Terrence would do something like this." She liked Terrence and had been deeply saddened when she found out that he had been stealing drugs from the hospital.

"Honey, you believe that there's good in everybody," Jerome said. "You didn't know that ol' boy was abusing drugs—no one really did until he started flying over the cuckoo's nest. He had it so bad that he was stealing the patients' medicine. I heard that he was switching out the meds for placebos."

Camille met Jerome's gaze. "Why do you listen to the rumor mill? Half of what you hear isn't true. I don't believe he was stealing his patients' medicine."

"Girl, you need to take off those rose-colored glasses."

Camille chuckled. "Jerome, you are so wrong." She clicked open her email in-box to check her email.

He shrugged. "Hey, it's true. You know that I'm right."

"Hey, I have an email from Mr. Wade," she announced. "He wants to meet with me today at some point."

Jerome surveyed her face. "You sound like this is a meeting you want to avoid. What's up with that?"

Camille had forgotten how well Jerome knew her. She had been at odds with Maxwell Wade since he was retained to represent Hopewell General. His arrogance had come through his email correspondence, irritating her. She had to deal with the arrogance of some of the male doctors on a daily basis and having Maxwell Wade around was just going to add one more sexist alpha male to the mix.

"Camille…" Jerome prompted.

"It's nothing," she said. "He just rubbed me the wrong way in a couple of his emails."

"If anybody can handle Maxwell Wade, it's you, Camille." Jerome checked his watch. "Well, it's time for me to start my day. I'll catch you later."

"Stay out of trouble, Jerome."

He laughed. "Not hardly. Especially if 'Miss Thang' has anything to do with it."

"You'd better not let Kayla hear you call her that," Camille warned. Kayla Tsang was the head nurse in Hopewell General's emergency room. Everyone called her Miss Thang behind her back. She was the one who kept a list of everyone's wrongs and reported them to the chief of staff.

Her words didn't faze Jerome. "Miss Thang knows when to back off me. Call me if you want to have a late lunch together."

"I will," she promised.

Camille checked her calendar. She then sent a quick email to Maxwell to let him know that she had some time before eleven to meet with him.

He responded quickly to confirm that he would come to her office at 10:00 a.m.

"Great," she whispered. Camille hoped the meeting would go smoothly. She had always been very easy to work with, but she was not about to let Maxwell order her around like some second-rate employee. Camille could tell by his emails that he was used to issuing orders. However, she would stand her ground if necessary.

Camille was able to respond to emails and send out a few of her own before her assistant announced, "Mr. Maxwell Wade is here to see you."

"Please give me a few minutes before you send him in, Lori." Camille wanted some time to mentally prepare for her meeting with the attorney.

Lori nodded and walked out of the office.

Five minutes later, she returned with Maxwell in tow.

Camille rose to her feet and walked around the desk. Maxwell Wade was as devilishly handsome as his photographs suggested, perhaps even more so in person.

She released a soft, cleansing breath and said, "It's nice to finally meet you in person."

Camille took in his powerful presence and drank in the sensuality of his physique. The man was *fine*. And those sexy warm brown eyes of his...they could make a woman melt just from the heat of his gaze.

She affected an ease she did not feel, but Camille was not about to give Maxwell any hint of how much he affected her.

Maxwell smiled as he shook her hand. "It is a pleasure to meet you, Camille." Her natural beauty had taken him by surprise.

Smiling, Camille gestured toward one of the visitor chairs in her office and said, "Please have a seat."

Maxwell sat down in the leather chair. He could not resist admiring her slender frame and soft curves. Although he preferred women with long hair, he liked the way her light brown, naturally wavy hair framed her face. Camille wore it in a cute short cut that complimented her *café-au-lait* skin color and green eyes.

Unaware that he was observing her, Camille strolled around her desk and sat down. "I didn't expect you here so soon, Mr. Wade. I was told that you wouldn't be settling in until Monday."

"I decided to come in a few days earlier so I can be here for Thomas's wedding reception," he responded. "Please call me Maxwell."

She had forgotten that Maxwell, Ray and Thomas had all been friends since college. Camille felt the heat of his gaze on her and shifted uncomfortably in her chair.

"I wanted to meet with you to discuss Dr. Matthews and his lawsuit," Maxwell announced.

"Because of the hospital's relationship with the Matthews family, we had hoped the matter with Terrence could be handled in a discreet manner," she responded. "We never expected a lawsuit to come out of the situation."

"No one ever expects a lawsuit, Camille," Maxwell stated bluntly. "In this case, I would have been more surprised if Dr. Matthews had gone away quietly."

His tone rubbed her the wrong way. "What I meant is that Terrence was caught red-handed with the drugs. How can he defend himself against the truth?"

"He can't," Maxwell responded. "An employee who wishes to sue for wrongful termination must either show that his employment contract expressly or implicitly stated that he would not be fired without cause or that the employer fired him for a reason that violates a fundamental policy expressed in Virginia's statutes. He could also sue if the employer committed some type of tort, like defamation, invasion of privacy or intentional infliction of emotional distress. But Dr. Matthews can't prove any of these things."

"Yet he's filed anyway," Camille commented.

Maxwell smiled. "Well, this is where I come in. From this point forward, all queries will be directed to me. No one here at the hospital is to talk to the media or anybody else."

"I'll forward a couple emails from reporters to you," Camille said.

"Great. I want you to know that I really appreciate your assistance, Camille."

His words warmed her. "Thank you."

"I will let you get back to work." Maxwell rose to his feet and headed to the door.

Up until recently, he and Camille had only exchanged a couple of pointed emails. He never expected to meet such a beautiful woman with a sinful voice and cute laugh. In her office, Maxwell had to concentrate hard just to keep his mind on business. Camille had made his temperature rise more than a little.

When Maxwell left her office, Camille leaned back in her chair and released a short sigh.

Maxwell Wade was gorgeous up close. She had to agree with Isabelle and the others. He did look even better in person. When he was in her office, Camille could barely concentrate and struggled to keep from staring at him.

There was a soft knock on her door, taking her attention off her thoughts of Maxwell Wade.

It was Jaclyn Campbell, the intern who had blown the whistle on Dr. Terrence Matthews.

"I just saw Maxwell Wade leaving your office," she said.

"Are you okay?" Camille inquired, noting that her friend looked upset about something.

"I still can't believe that Terrence and his family are suing the hospital," Jaclyn said as she sat down in one of the visitor chairs. "How can he claim he was wrongfully terminated?"

"I know how you feel," Camille responded. "I can't believe it either, Jaclyn."

"I just wish we could find a way to lay this lawsuit to rest. I overheard a couple of patients discussing it."

Camille shook her head. "I've been doing everything I can to keep the hospital out of the news, but Terrence and his parents calling that press conference didn't help matters at all."

"I feel terrible that it's come to this," Jaclyn murmured.

"It's not your fault," Camille stated. "Terrence did this. And his claim that his termination was extreme is certainly not true."

"His family is one of the richest families in all of Virginia."

"And the hospital's most generous benefactor," Camille interjected. "The fact remains that there was sufficient grounds to terminate Terrence, and with Maxwell Wade representing the hospital, I'm sure he'll sort out the whole mess."

Camille got up to walk Jaclyn out of her office.

"So what do you think of Maxwell Wade?" Jaclyn inquired.

Camille met her friend's gaze. "I think he's arrogant, but maybe this is why he's so good at his job."

"He's nice-looking, don't you think?"

"Jaclyn, why are you asking me about him? The one

you should be talking to is your former roommate. She's already put her claim on him."

"He's not Isabelle's type," Jaclyn responded.

"I'm pretty sure she'd disagree with you," Camille stated. "Anyway, your focus should be on Dr. Lucien De Winter."

Jaclyn smiled. "He has all of my attention, I assure you."

Camille was happy that her friend had found a wonderful man who loved her as much as she loved him. As for herself, she enjoyed her life as a single woman, but she was willing to settle down if and when the right man came along.

Chapter 2

Dr. Thomas Bradshaw and his new wife, Lia, mingled with their guests during the reception held in their honor. The couple had eloped, surprising everyone, including Camille. Lia radiated happiness as her husband embraced her lovingly.

Camille moved around the room, pausing to chat with friends and coworkers.

She walked over to where Lucien and his fiancée Jaclyn stood. "How come you two aren't out there dancing?"

"Every time we head out there, Lucien gets sidetracked by one of the board members," Jaclyn stated.

Lucien embraced her. "I'm sorry, sweetheart. When the next song plays, I'm all yours."

"What about you, Camille?" Jaclyn asked. "Why aren't you out there dancing?"

"My imaginary date is shy," she responded with a laugh.

They were soon joined by Tamara St. John and her fiancé, Victor Aguilar; both were interns at Hopewell General. Camille talked with them for a moment before moving on.

She caught sight of Maxwell standing with Ray a few feet away. Her breath caught in her throat at the sight of him in the black suit that looked as if it had been designed just for him. It was obvious why he had so many women fawning over him. Camille couldn't deny that Maxwell was a very handsome man.

Her eyes traveled across the room to where Isabelle stood with a couple of her friends. Camille noted that she had been watching Maxwell along with half of the other women at the reception.

"Camille, why are you over here in this corner?" Jerome asked, approaching her. "Wallflower definitely does not look good on you."

His words cut into her thoughts of Maxwell.

She laughed. "Jerome, I'm not trying to be a wallflower."

He set his drink on a nearby table and grabbed her by the hand. "C'mon, let's dance then."

"What about your date?" Camille inquired. "You know that I don't do drama."

"She'll be all right. I told Julie that you were like a little sister to me. Besides, she's not the jealous type."

Camille loved to dance, so as soon as she heard the music, her body began to sway.

She and Jerome danced to two songs before his date joined them. Camille stayed on the floor for one more song, and then said, "Okay, I need to get something to drink."

"You're leaving?" Jerome asked. "I was about to drop it like it's hot."

She laughed. "I'll leave that to you and Julie."

Camille made her way over to the bar.

Someone walked up behind her.

"Hello, Camille."

She turned around. "Maxwell, it's nice to see you," she managed casually. Camille could hear her heart pounding loudly over the music. His nearness had an arousing effect on her. "I hope you're having a good time."

"I am," he responded in a deep baritone voice.

A new and unexpected warmth surged through her as he looked at her. The richness of his tone made Camille weak at the knees. She supported her weight by placing a hand on the edge of the bar.

She could feel Maxwell's eyes still observing her. His gaze was intense and penetrating, almost as if he could see right through her. Camille chewed nervously on her bottom lip.

Jerome walked by and uttered, "Stop biting your lip."

Embarrassed, Camille gave him a playful jab in the ribs. She prayed that Maxwell hadn't heard him.

Her prayer went unanswered when Maxwell smiled at her, and then asked, "Do I make you nervous, Camille?"

"No," she responded quickly. "Why would you think that?"

Camille couldn't stand his arrogance. Did he actually believe that her actions were because of him?

"Most people bite their lips when anxious or nervous."

Camille gestured to the dance floor. "Why aren't

you out there?" She wanted to take the attention off of herself.

"That's one of the reasons I walked over here," Maxwell responded. "I came over to ask you to dance with me."

She caught sight of Isabelle standing a few yards away and was about to refuse, but he said, "I saw you out there with your coworker. You have some really nice moves. I thought maybe you could teach me a few."

She folded her arms across her chest. "Okay, now you're just teasing me."

He gave her a beautiful smile. "I'm serious. Come, let's have some fun."

Why not? "Sure."

They slowly made their way to the middle of the dance floor.

She wasn't surprised to find that Maxwell was a wonderful dancer. Camille smiled as she showed off her best moves, wanting to prove that he wasn't the only one with skills.

"You enjoy dancing, don't you?"

Smiling, she nodded. "You look like you love it as well."

"I'm going to tell you a secret." He leaned forward and whispered in her ear. His words made her grin.

Later when they walked off the dance floor, Camille couldn't resist asking, "Were you serious about wanting to dance professionally?"

Maxwell nodded. "It used to be a dream of mine, but my parents insisted that I find a real profession. They didn't believe that dancing would pay the bills."

"Is that why you became a lawyer?"

He nodded. "My parents and grandfather are all lawyers, so I felt that I should carry on the family tradition."

"Being a lawyer has served you well, wouldn't you say?" Camille questioned. Maxwell was one of the top litigation attorneys in the country. He was licensed to practice in California, New York, D.C., Virginia and Georgia.

He smiled. "I can't complain."

She spotted Isabelle walking toward them and said, "Thanks for the dance, Maxwell."

He smiled at her. "You're quite welcome, Camille."

"Mr. Wade," Isabelle said, joining them. "Let's dance. Camille, you don't mind if I take him off your hands, do you?"

He shot a glance in Camille's direction.

"Have fun," she mouthed before weaving through the sea of people in attendance.

Camille watched as Maxwell allowed Isabelle to take him by the hand, leading him to the dance floor. She had mixed emotions as she watched the two of them dancing.

Even in a crowd, Maxwell's presence was compelling. Camille stood there eyeing the numerous women vying for his attention.

"Isabelle's really trying to latch on to him," a woman standing beside her commented in a low voice.

Camille did not respond. She liked Isabelle, although she felt that Isabelle was all wrong for a man like Maxwell Wade. Not that she knew what type of woman was perfect for the millionaire attorney. Besides, he had been linked to a flamboyant supermodel for years, a woman who was rumored to be self-centered, hard to work with, and ill-tempered. She had earned a reputation for gaining attention through public tantrums, including an attack on her assistant, during her on-and-off relationship with Maxwell.

Camille allowed her eyes to linger on Maxwell, appreciating the strong lines of his well-formed cheek and jaw. But it was those beautiful brown eyes of his that arrested her—intelligent eyes that seemed to peer through to her very soul. She surveyed Maxwell with an artist's sensitivity, taking in his naturally arched brows, the faint lines above his forehead and those sexy lips of his.

"What do you think about Isabelle and Maxwell Wade, Camille?"

She gave a slight shrug. "I think that Isabelle's a big girl and she can take care of herself," Camille responded. "Hey, I'm going to get something to drink. Want to join me?"

"My boyfriend just went to get drinks for us," the woman replied. "Thanks though."

Camille nodded, and then said, "I'll talk to you later." She was grateful for a moment alone. She struggled with figuring out what was drawing her to Maxwell. There was some type of invisible thread drawing them together.

I don't know this man, she kept telling herself over and over. *I'm not sure I even like him, so why should I care who he dates?*

Camille shook off her thoughts.

She ordered and paid the bartender for a soda.

Just as she turned to leave, Camille bumped into the chief of staff's wife. "Mrs. Dudley, I'm sorry. I didn't know that you were standing behind me."

"You're fine, dear." She placed a hand to her forehead. "I have such a terrible headache and this music isn't helping. I can barely see straight, so I'm going home."

She was genuinely concerned. "I'm sorry to hear

that, Mrs. Dudley. Would you like for me to call you a taxi or something?"

"Germaine's already taken care of it, dear."

Dr. Dudley was in heavy conversation with another doctor, so Camille made sure that the woman made it safely to the waiting taxi.

Just before she reached the doors of the ballroom where the reception was being held, Dr. Dudley stepped into her path. "D-did my w-wife leave?" he asked. The dazed look in his eyes and the slur in his voice indicated that he had had plenty to drink.

"Yes," Camille responded. "I walked her out to the cab myself."

He reached over and grabbed her hand. "Thank you for being so kind to my wife." Dr. Dudley was close enough for Camille to smell the alcohol on his breath— much too close as far as she was concerned.

Camille took a step backward and tried to remove her hand from Dudley's viselike grip.

He stared at her a moment before saying, "I really love those green eyes of yours. It gives you an exotic look."

She didn't like the way he was caressing her with his eyes.

"Dr. Dudley," Camille began. "Why don't we go inside?"

"I'm actually en-enjoying myself out here," he said in response. "There are too many people inside the party. I've wanted to just sit down and talk to you for a while, Camille. I like getting to know my employees."

"I believe we know each other as well as we need to," she stated firmly. "Dr. Dudley, we don't want people walking out here and making assumptions. The hospital is under enough scrutiny, don't you think?"

Camille tried a second time unsuccessfully to pull her hand away, but Dudley only held on tighter. A wave of apprehension washed over her. "Please let my hand go, Doctor."

He continued to leer at her. "Hey, I'm just trying to get to know you—with your fine self."

Camille had heard rumors that Dudley had an eye for the ladies, and on more than one occasion she had caught him staring at her, but she never thought he would be so blatant with it. Dr. Dudley was not only married, but a father of three and well-respected in the medical field.

"Why don't we go get you some coffee?" Camille suggested. "You have been drinking all night and the alcohol's making you do things I'm sure you will regret."

He pulled her into his arms and tried to kiss her.

"No!"

Cringing, Camille struggled violently in his arms, and was relieved when he abruptly let her go. She opened her eyes and met Maxwell's hard gaze.

Mortified, she looked away and straightened her dress.

"Dudley, I think Camille's right. You've had enough to drink," Maxwell stated coldly.

"I'm...I'm f-fine," Germaine slurred. "Now...if you would excuse us, I'm try...t-trying to have a conversation with Camille."

"I'm perfectly aware of what you are trying to do," he countered. "It's time for you to go home, so I'm going to call you a taxi." Maxwell pulled out his cell phone. He gestured to a passing waiter and said, "Could you please bring this man a cup of black coffee?"

He glanced back at Camille. "Are you okay?"

"I just need to get out of here," she murmured.

Maxwell nodded in understanding. He could tell that she was really shaken by what had just transpired. "I'll see you to your car once I get Dudley settled."

Camille sat down in one of the chairs across from where he and Dudley were.

She couldn't hear what Maxwell was saying to Dudley, but from the expression on his face, the conversation was an intense one.

Maxwell stayed with Dudley until the taxi arrived. Just as she had done with Dudley's wife, he escorted the chief of staff outside.

"C'mon, I'll see you to your car," Maxwell said when he returned.

"I didn't drive. I came with one of the nurses. I'll just call a taxi."

"You don't have to do that," he told her. "I'll drive you home."

"Maxwell, I appreciate your help with Dr. Dudley, but you don't have to go out of your way to drive me to my place."

"I don't mind," Maxwell responded. "After the night you've had, I want to make sure that you get home safe."

It wasn't until Camille was inside her townhome that she allowed her tears to flow. She always enjoyed entering her home, where the pride of ownership was evident. Camille had paid great attention to detail in the remodeled kitchen, which included granite countertops and upgraded appliances. The hardwood floors throughout both stories gleamed to perfection.

However, tonight her efforts were wasted on herself. She rushed up the stairs and into her bedroom, where she quickly removed her clothes and stepped into the shower.

She felt dirty all over.

She scrubbed her hands until they were sore. Camille wanted to erase the memory of Dr. Dudley's touch.

Afterward, Camille had hoped that watching television would help to ease her mind, but it didn't. She couldn't stop thinking about what happened.

I'm so glad Maxwell was there. I don't know what would've happened if he had not intervened when he did.

A wave of anger coursed through her veins and she silently debated whether or not to have a conversation with the chief of staff on Monday morning.

Camille picked up a pillow and angrily tossed it across the room.

When did I morph into a knight in shining armor? Maxwell wondered as he drove back to his hotel.

Normally, he would've never let such a beautiful woman walk away without so much as a kiss. Most of his goodbyes ended at dawn. Maxwell hadn't missed the pain and fear that shined bright in Camille's eyes. She looked terrified of what she was facing and his heart felt for her.

Camille was in such a fragile state of mind, Matthew thought it better just to make sure she got home safe. He would never do what Dr. Dudley had tried to do.

A wave of anger coursed through Maxwell. He was furious with Dudley and planned to have a long conversation with him. The chief of staff was not only placing his career in jeopardy, but the reputation of the hospital as well. If he didn't keep his hands or comments to himself, Hopewell General would find itself in the midst of a huge sexual harassment lawsuit. The hospital had enough legal problems already.

Fifteen minutes later, Maxwell strolled into the beautifully appointed lobby of Morrison House, a hotel surrounded by the historic neighborhood of Old Town Alexandria. He loved the classic American redbrick building that housed the four-star hotel where he would be staying during his time in Virginia.

Maxwell stifled a yawn. He was more than ready to dive into the four-poster bed in his suite. He unlocked and opened the door to a room decorated with a soothing color scheme of golds, creams and cranberry reds with accents of forest green.

He strolled to the adjoining parlor and laid his keys to the rental car on the writing desk. Maxwell's thoughts traveled back to Camille and how stunning she had looked in her black dress.

His cell phone rang, cutting into his thoughts.

"Hello, Kendra." Maxwell hid his irritation. Although they were no longer seeing each other, she still had a way of getting under his skin and not in a good way. He had finally had the good sense to end things for good.

"Hey, baby. How are you?"

"I'm fine," Maxwell responded dryly. "Why aren't you out somewhere with your posse?" he asked, referring to the camera crew that followed her around.

Kendra released an audible sigh. "Maxwell, I know how much you hate my doing this reality show, but, baby, I have to think about my career. I am worth so much more now because of it."

"It's intrusive."

"I have nothing to hide," Kendra stated. "I'm a celebrity supermodel. People want to know all about my life. At least I make money by inviting my fans into my world. Hey, the network is considering doing another reality show to help me find Mr. Right. I told them that I've already found the perfect man for me."

"Kendra…" Maxwell began.

She cut him off by saying, "Baby, I love you and I know that you love me, too."

"Now you're telling me what I feel?"

"Are you saying that you don't have feelings for me?" she inquired.

"Kendra, I care about you, but you know what we had is over. We've talked about this more than once." He was growing tired of having the same discussion over and over.

"Maxwell, I don't believe we're over," Kendra argued. "Don't you remember how good we were together?"

He shook his head and sighed in resignation. Once Kendra made her mind up, there was no changing it.

"When are you coming home?"

"Not for another week or two."

"I miss you, Maxwell."

"I'm surprised you have time to miss me or anyone else. You've been pretty busy with the show and your public appearances."

"We could be filmed while on a romantic date," Kendra suggested.

"No," Malcolm stated. "I told you from the beginning that I wanted nothing to do with that show of yours, Kendra, and I meant it."

"People want to see me with the man I love."

"I can't help you."

"You mean you *won't* help me," she countered.

"Kendra, I don't want to argue with you. I'm tired and I have a breakfast meeting in the morning. I'll talk to you later."

She slammed the phone down in his ear.

Her actions no longer fazed Maxwell. He and Kendra had been in and out of a relationship for years and he was tired of the cycle. It was time for something new, as far as he was concerned. There were scores of beautiful women in the world—too many to settle for Kendra's drama.

An image of Camille formed in his mind.

Maxwell was concerned about her, but he hadn't thought to ask Camille for her home or cell number. He would just have to wait until Monday to see how she was doing.

Maxwell wondered how Camille would interact with Dr. Dudley after what happened earlier in the evening. From a legal standpoint, Hopewell didn't need any hint of a sexual harassment lawsuit. However, harassment, in any form, was never to be tolerated.

The decision to file a complaint was solely Camille's, but he hoped to avoid another scandal while dealing with the Matthews case. Ray had already consulted him on another pending lawsuit in which the hospital admitted fault in giving a patient the wrong medication. Yes, the last thing Hopewell needed was a sexual harassment lawsuit.

However, he vowed to support Camille in whatever she decided.

Chapter 3

Camille had planned to do some Christmas shopping that weekend, but after what happened last night with Dr. Dudley, she decided to stay home. She was still too shaken to be around a crowd of people. Right now she desired to stay in the security of her cozy two-bedroom townhome.

She spent most of the morning researching sexual harassment, although she wasn't sure filing a complaint was the right move to make. Dr. Dudley clearly had had too much to drink last night, so most likely it was the alcohol talking. But then, this wasn't the first time he'd made sexual innuendoes. She had heard comments from Isabelle and some of the other interns about Dudley, but she had chosen to believe that he was harmless until recently.

She had always been accused of believing that there was good in every human being. Camille wanted to believe it, but the actions of her chief of staff left her with doubt. She had heard the rumors about him and Nurse Tsang, but had dismissed them as nonsense, especially since Dudley had instituted a non-fraternization policy in the hospital. Nurses and interns—even the doctors themselves—often gossiped.

Dudley appeared to be a happily married man, although his wife and children traveled frequently to visit family. However, if the rumors were true, Camille could not understand why he would resort to extramarital affairs when he had such a lovely wife at home.

Camille was torn.

She didn't want to say anything out of her affection for Mrs. Dudley and the children. Perhaps she should sit down with the chief and try to get him to see the error of his ways. Camille didn't want to bring the hospital board into this or subject the hospital to more legal action.

By the late afternoon, Camille decided to go to the gym. Whenever she was frustrated, she liked to play a game of basketball. Usually on Saturdays, there was a co-ed game going on in her neighborhood.

Camille really needed to release some of the tension she felt. If Maxwell hadn't come along when he did, she had no idea how far Dr. Dudley would have gone.

Even now, she wasn't sure how she would handle facing her chief of staff on Monday. He had once been a man she respected. Now, whenever she thought of him, Camille felt repulsed.

Maxwell decided to get some of his Christmas shopping out of the way. He wanted to pick up a few gifts for his nieces and nephew especially. He spent the greater part of Saturday afternoon in Landmark Mall, and then met Ray for an early dinner.

"So what do you think of Camille Hunter?" Ray asked while they were waiting for their food to arrive.

"She's a nice girl," Maxwell responded with a slight shrug. "Why do you ask?"

"I saw you two on the dance floor last night." He grinned. "The two of you looked pretty good together. Camille is a real sweetheart."

He gave his friend a sidelong look. "You wouldn't be trying to set me up with her, would you, Ray?"

Feigning innocence, Ray responded, "Naw…just thought you might be interested in her. That's all."

"She is beautiful," Maxwell admitted. "But I didn't come to Virginia to find a girlfriend or a wife. Once we get this case settled, I'm heading back to New York."

Ray took a sip of his iced tea before inquiring, "Are you still in contact with Kendra?"

Maxwell nodded. "She refuses to accept that our relationship is over. I've told her over and over again, but it doesn't seem to sink in."

"Maybe it isn't really over," Ray suggested. "You two have broken up and gotten back together so many times, I've lost count."

The waiter arrived with their meals.

Maxwell waited until he left before saying, "I used to believe that Kendra was the only woman for me."

"What changed your mind?"

He met Ray's gaze. "It took me a while, but I eventually realized that no relationship should be that hard or that dramatic. When Kendra doesn't get her way, she goes out and does something crazy. Take this reality show for example. She wants to air our problems to the entire world and she expects me to be okay with it."

Ray chuckled. "She does talk about you a lot on the show."

"You actually watch it?" Maxwell asked. He sliced off a piece of his steak and stuck it in his mouth, chewing slowly.

"You've never watched it?" Ray asked. He wiped his mouth on the edge of his napkin.

Maxwell shook his head. "I don't intend to watch the show ever, but then I am not a fan of reality shows. I actually find it strange that all of the celebrities I've come into contact with complain of not having any privacy—yet half of them are now starring in reality shows."

Ray agreed.

The two men finished off their meals while discussing the Matthews lawsuit.

After Ray paid the check, he asked, "So what are you getting into this evening?"

Maxwell checked his watch. "I'm tired so I'm going to head back to the hotel. I'll see you on Monday morning."

"Bright and early," Ray added. "We're finishing up the depositions next week."

"Good," Maxwell said. "I'd like to review all of them as soon as possible."

They parted ways with Maxwell heading back to the hotel to review the Matthews case file, and Ray on his way to meet his girlfriend.

Camille entered his thoughts once more. Maxwell could understand why Dr. Dudley found her attractive. He thought she was beautiful as well.

I really love her green eyes and her gorgeous smile.

Maxwell gave himself a mental shake. He and Camille were coworkers. He had vowed a long time ago to keep romance and work separated.

* * *

Monday morning arrived much too early for Camille.

For the first time in her career, she dreaded going to Hopewell General. Seeing Dr. Dudley and Maxwell Wade would only force her to relive one of the more embarrassing moments of her life.

Camille was thankful to Maxwell for rescuing her, but she was unhappy to be even a little in his debt.

She was glad that no one was around when she entered the hospital. She just needed some time alone before she started work. However, as soon as she stepped off the elevator on the second floor, she found Maxwell waiting for her inside the public relations office.

"Good morning," she greeted him and pasted on a smile, trying to depict an ease she did not feel.

"Do you have a moment?" he asked.

She was acutely aware of her assistant watching her interaction with Maxwell. She nodded and responded, "Sure, come into my office."

Maxwell followed her inside and closed the door behind them.

"How are you doing?" he asked.

Camille sank down in her chair. "I'm okay."

He didn't look like he believed her. She wasn't acting her usual self, although what could she expect? "Are you sure?" he asked.

Camille nodded. "Dr. Dudley was drunk the other night. Otherwise he wouldn't have behaved that way."

"Has he ever approached you in that manner before?" Maxwell wanted to know.

"Not really," Camille answered. "He has made some comments that I deemed inappropriate, but I'm sure he's harmless."

"Do you know if he's done this with other employees?"

"Maxwell, I've heard a few comments here and there that he has an eye for the ladies, but that's about it."

"I am going to have a talk with Dudley because the hospital doesn't need another scandal."

Camille couldn't read his expression, but his tone clearly indicated that Maxwell wasn't pleased by the actions of Hopewell's chief of staff.

"I don't think he really means any harm," she stated.

"Regardless, he needs to take precautions to protect the integrity of the hospital. No employee should have to deal with harassment of any kind, Camille. I just want to make sure that Dudley understands this."

"Maxwell, I don't want what happened at the party to get out."

"Neither do I," he confessed. "But I do intend to make sure it never happens again, especially on my watch."

His words gave Camille comfort. She knew that he was sincere and it touched her. Maxwell was so good-looking and charming that it unnerved her. "Thank you."

"You're welcome, Camille. If you need to talk, feel free to come to me."

"I'll be fine."

The gesture was a sweet one, but Camille would never unburden herself on a man like Maxwell. It was not like they were friends or anything. However, she didn't want to confide in Jerome where Dudley was concerned. Mostly because Jerome would go ballistic and she didn't want him losing his job over her.

Maxwell eyed her for a moment, and then smiled. "I don't doubt that for a moment."

His smile warmed her all over. Camille forced her attention from his perfectly shaped lips that could only be described as kissable. She had a lot to do and with Maxwell in her office, all she could do was think about him. After a moment, she said, "Have a good day, Maxwell."

She leaned back in her chair, secretly admiring the way his navy blazer fit his muscular build.

"You, too."

When he left her office, Camille released a soft sigh. Why on earth did the man have such a strong effect on her?

Dr. Dudley appeared in her doorway, forcing her out of her reverie. Camille stiffened in her chair.

"Do you have a minute to talk?" he asked. The doctor looked just as uncomfortable as she did.

Camille nodded, unable to get the words out.

"I wanted to apologize for my actions the other night," he said sheepishly. "I had a lot to drink and I guess I lost my head for a moment. Camille, I want you to know that what happened…well, it won't happen again. I give you my word."

"Dr. Dudley, your apology is accepted," Camille responded with no emotion. She wanted to say more—to yell at him for his actions—but she held back. However, she vowed if he ever crossed the line again, she would file a formal complaint. The hospital was already under fire for the actions of another doctor. Camille wanted to spare Hopewell General of another scandal.

He gave a slight nod and walked briskly out of her office.

Although she appreciated the gesture, Dr. Dudley's apology did nothing to relieve Camille's apprehension. She wasn't sure if she would ever feel safe around him again.

* * *

Maxwell had wanted to comfort Camille.

To tell the truth, he wanted to make love to her.

What is going on with me? Maxwell wondered. He hadn't experienced such a strong connection to a woman in a long time. Camille was not even his type, which was why this was so puzzling to him.

She looked professional in her conservative, navy blue pant suit with a pair of comfortable pumps.

Ray had just arrived when Maxwell walked out of Camille's office.

"Your office is set up and ready for you," he told Maxwell. "We have a conference call scheduled with Matthews's attorney at eleven."

"Sounds good," Maxwell said. He was more than ready to get this lawsuit settled so that he could return to New York. As far as he was concerned, this particular case presented no challenge to him, and would be resolved quickly.

Maxwell settled into his office.

He set down at his desk and made a few phone calls. The first was to his secretary in New York and the second was to his father. They were working together on a case that was due to go to trial in the spring of next year.

Maxwell made notes during his conversation with his father.

"Thanks, Dad," he said. "Fax me a copy of the interrogatories when you get them."

They talked for a few minutes more before hanging up.

"Knock. Knock."

Maxwell glanced up from his notes. "Isabelle. Come in." He remembered being introduced to her at the reception. He had to admit that Ray was right. She looked like she could be Jennifer Lopez's twin.

She walked inside, carrying a medium-size plant. "I thought your office could use some brightening up."

He smiled. "Thank you, Isabelle. That was very sweet of you."

"It needs lots of light, so I'll put it over here," she was saying.

The scent of her perfume was distracting—mostly because it was the same scent that Kendra wore.

"How are you enjoying our city?" Isabelle asked.

"It's nice," he replied. "I've always liked Alexandria."

Isabelle gave him a sexy grin. "Really?"

"It's nice here and I love exploring the rich history, but I'm a New Yorker for life." He noted a flash of disappointment in her eyes. Maxwell didn't want to give her false hope.

"Ray mentioned that you were thinking about going into pediatrics," Maxwell stated.

She nodded. "I love children."

He leaned back in his chair. "Since you're here, I'd like to talk to you about Terrence Matthews."

"Okay," she responded. "What do you want to know?"

"Did you ever notice anything that you considered odd behavior?" Maxwell asked.

"There were a couple of times that he didn't seem quite himself, but I thought it was because he was tired. We work some pretty long hours from time to time. Oh yeah, he did miss a couple of staff meetings, but I've missed one before. Time can get away from you."

Maxwell played with his pen. "So you never suspected that he was abusing drugs?"

"No, I didn't. To be honest, I was shocked when I heard that he was stealing them from the hospital."

Maxwell silently noted that almost everyone had the same sentiment. He'd read many of the witness statements over the weekend. Terrence Matthews was apparently a functioning drug user.

She ran her fingers through her hair. "Do you have any more questions for me?"

He went over his notes. "This is it for now."

"Well, I've kept you from your work long enough," Isabelle said with a short laugh. "I want you to know that we're really glad you're here. This hospital needs someone like you in our corner."

Maxwell pushed away from his desk and stood up. He knew that Isabelle was vying for his attention, but he was not attracted to her, although he considered her extremely beautiful.

"Thank you for speaking with me, Isabelle. Everything we discussed will remain confidential."

"I'm not worried," she told him. "I like Dr. Matthews, but what he's doing to this hospital is wrong."

"Thank you for the plant as well."

She glanced up at him, smiling. "It was my pleasure, Mr. Wade."

"Call me Maxwell," he told her.

"Sure thing."

He laughed. "I'll walk you out."

Maxwell wasn't sure what happened next, but the next thing he realized she was falling. Reacting quickly, he reached out to grab her.

Camille eyed the calendar and decided that since today was Maxwell Wade's first official day at Hopewell General, she should do something nice for him. He had not only protected her from Dr. Dudley, but had gone out of his way to make sure that she was okay.

She left her office before she could change her mind about asking him to have lunch with her.

Camille's pace halted at the presence of Isabelle Morales in Maxwell's arms when she arrived at his office.

Camille was astounded. He had been in the hospital for less than a day and already had one of the interns in his arms.

She sent Isabelle a sharp look. Camille couldn't believe that her coworker would behave so blatantly.

Without a word, she returned to her office in a huff.

The thought of Maxwell getting involved with Isabelle bothered Camille to the core, as much as she hated to admit it. She had to sheathe her inner feelings as a sense of inadequacy swept over her.

A few minutes later, Maxwell appeared in her doorway.

"You ran off before I could explain."

"You don't owe me any explanation," Camille responded stiffly.

"What you saw back there…it's not what it looked like."

She met his gaze. "You really don't have to explain anything to me. Who or what you do in this hospital is not my concern. However, you should at least close the door. Especially after the conversation we had this morning about sexual harassment. I can't believe you would place yourself and Dr. Morales in a position to be gossiped about."

"Isabelle…Dr. Morales was about to fall. There—"

Camille interrupted him by saying, "We need to block out some time to discuss the legal issues the hospital is dealing with. If it's okay with you, I'll email you with a time to meet."

"That's fine," Maxwell said. "Is that why you were coming to see me?"

"Yes," she lied.

Camille picked up her phone, silently dismissing him. She was aware of Maxwell watching her, but pretended not to notice that his presence had overtaken her office.

He stood there for a moment in silence, then turned on his heel and left.

Camille waited until she was positive that Maxwell was gone before hanging up. She wasn't really planning to make a call; she just wanted him to leave her office.

"Isabelle was right," she whispered. "She said he wouldn't be alone for long."

She really liked Isabelle, but for some reason, Camille did not like the idea of her friend getting involved with Maxwell. After all, Maxwell seemed to enjoy his life as a bachelor. He was often linked with actresses or socialites when he and Kendra weren't involved. Camille didn't want to see Isabelle get her heart broken.

She didn't want to consider that there could be another reason why she didn't want to see Isabelle with Maxwell.

Chapter 4

Maxwell found his little exchange with Camille humorous.

He was delighted at the thought of her being jealous. He wasn't sure why the thought pleased him, but it did. It thrilled him that Camille wasn't immune to him like he had originally assumed.

He spotted his friend Thomas and another doctor, Lucien De Winter, talking in an office. Thomas gestured for Maxwell to join them.

"Lucien was just telling me about Dudley and how he's trying to make life difficult for him and Jaclyn since their engagement."

"He's also harassing Victor Aguilar and Tamara St. John," Lucien stated. "They just recently got engaged."

"I'm not a fan of non-fraternization policies," Maxwell interjected. "I think the workplace is one of the logical locations for people to meet and fall in love, as long as the employees engaged in the relationship follow common-sense guidelines."

"I agree," Lucien said. "The employees have asked him to remove the ban on fraternization for years, but Dudley refuses. He and his watchdog, Nurse Tsang, are making everyone miserable."

"The only thing I've agreed with Dudley on is how he handled Terrence," Thomas confessed. "Although I appreciate all he did for me and Lia."

"Lucien, I'd like to speak with you about Dr. Matthews," Maxwell said. "If you have another minute, I want to ask you some questions."

"Sure."

Thomas made his way to the door. "I need to make my rounds, so I'll call you later, Maxwell."

"What can you tell me about Dr. Matthews, Lucien?"

"He was a promising doctor with a bedside manner that all of his patients appreciated." Lucien shook his head sadly. "If only we could have found a way to help him."

"Did you notice anything?"

Lucien nodded. "He was no longer as reliable. For example, he used to be the first one to arrive at staff meetings, but then he was either late or a no-show. He was also the doctor who gave that patient the wrong medication. Because of his family, Dudley made sure that was never made public."

"What steps did you take at that point?" Maxwell questioned.

"We had Terrence take a drug test, although we had a witness to him stealing the drugs. His test came back positive. Terrence maintains that we faked the results, however. He has had some independent tests done and the results show that he's clean."

"Do you think he paid someone to change the results?"

"Or take the test for him," Lucien offered. "When I asked Terrence about the charges, he never denied them. He didn't feel the need to deny them as his family was the hospital's biggest benefactor."

"He was offered the chance to go into rehab?"

Lucien nodded. "He flat-out refused. He would probably still have his job if he had taken a medical leave and gone into rehab. When he didn't, we had no choice but to let him go."

Maxwell opened his mouth to speak, but before he could get the words out, Lucien's pager went off.

"I'm sorry but I have to leave."

Maxwell opened the door to the office. "Thanks for your time."

He walked out after Lucien and returned to his own office. For a split second, Maxwell considered going back to Camille's office.

She was right.

Although he and Isabelle were innocent of any wrongdoing, had someone walked by his office, they could have easily drawn the wrong conclusions. Worse, Isabelle could accuse him of sexual harassment, although he doubted she would make such a claim.

Seated at his desk, Maxwell went through his list of witnesses. There were still several he wanted to speak with. He preferred doing his own interviews and not just relying on statements. Body language often presented the real story.

He tried to keep his mind on his work, but an image of Camille kept popping up in his head.

She was jealous.

It surprised and pleased him that she was attracted

to him. However, Maxwell felt like he had been doused with a bucket of ice water when he realized that the attraction was mutual.

Camille tried to concentrate on her work, but couldn't. She was furious with herself for allowing Maxwell Wade to get under her skin.

She picked up the apple on her desk and bit into it.

"Hey, there you are," a woman's voice called. "I came by here earlier and you were gone. I wanted to see if you had time to have lunch with me."

Camille looked up and saw Tamara St. John walking into her office. "I didn't know you were working today, Tamara," she said. She tossed the apple into the trash. "Sure. This apple really wasn't doing it for me."

"What's wrong?"

"Nothing," Camille responded. "Why do you ask?"

"Something's bothering you," Tamara said. "You look upset."

"I'm fine. I just need to get away from this place for a little while." Camille rose to her feet and grabbed her purse.

They left the hospital.

Camille and Tamara walked across the street to the restaurant frequented by most of the hospital staff.

"So, you're still not going to tell me what's got you so preoccupied?" Tamara asked after they were seated.

Camille smiled at her friend. "I'm fine, really."

"I hear we have the renowned Maxwell Wade helping the legal department. Have you met him?"

She nodded.

"So what do you think of him?" Tamara inquired.

"I don't really have an opinion of Mr. Wade," Camille lied. "I guess we'll really have to wait and see if he's as good as everyone says he is."

"He's very handsome from what I understand."

"That seems to be the consensus," Camille muttered. The last thing she wanted to do was spend her lunch hour discussing the arrogant Maxwell Wade. Changing the subject, she asked, "So have you and Victor decided on a wedding date?"

"We're still narrowing down dates."

Camille picked up her menu. "Just so you know…I don't do pastels."

Tamara laughed.

While waiting for their food, Camille scanned the dining area. The restaurant was a favorite of hospital employees and as usual it was filled with interns, doctors, nurses and other hospital staff. There were only a few people that she did not recognize.

The restaurant was not only convenient, it was warm and inviting. The soft lighting and beautiful artwork in vivid hues added to its charm. Fresh flowers on the tables welcomed every diner.

"Have you spoken to Terrence since the lawsuit?" Tamara asked in a low voice.

Camille shook her head no. "I thought he would contact me at some point, but he hasn't."

When their food arrived, Camille stabbed a fried shrimp and stuck it in her mouth. She loved shrimp.

"All my girl friends are engaged," she said. "I hope when you and Jaclyn get married, we will still be able to have our monthly girls' night out."

"For sure," Tamara said. "We're just getting married—not going to prison."

The two women shared a laugh.

"Seriously, though," Camille said. "I'm going to be the only single one left."

"Not for long," Tamara predicted. She wiped her mouth on the edge of her napkin.

"I don't know," Camille responded. "I want a man who will treat me like a queen. I want a man who will adore me, and most of the men I've met seem to be lacking in those areas."

Laughing, Tamara sliced off a piece of grilled catfish, piercing it with her fork.

Camille glanced across the room just as Maxwell and Thomas entered the restaurant.

Tamara turned, following Camille's gaze. "He's very handsome."

She didn't respond.

"You have to be blind not to notice that man," Tamara said as she turned her attention back to her meal. "I noticed that he couldn't seem to take his eyes off you."

"What are you talking about?" she asked.

Tamara eyed her. "You didn't notice the way he kept staring at you as he walked to his table?"

Camille shook her head. "He was most likely looking at you. You are more his type than I am."

"No, I'm pretty sure he was looking at you."

Shrugging, Camille responded, "It really doesn't matter. Maxwell and I live in two very different worlds."

"The thing that bothers me the most about the non-fraternization policy is that Dr. Dudley is a hypocrite," Thomas was saying.

"What do you mean by that?" Maxwell picked up his menu and began scanning the entrées. He stole a peek over to where Camille was sitting with her friend.

"Dudley is sleeping with one of the staff nurses,"

Thomas announced in a low voice. "Kayla Tsang to be exact."

Maxwell stiffened in shock. "Do you know this for sure, or is this just another hospital rumor?"

"This is no rumor," Thomas responded. "I saw them myself one night in his office."

"Apparently he's not just having an affair," Maxwell stated. "I know for a fact that he has been harassing some of the female staff. Just before lunch, an intern came to me upset. She asked me if she could pursue a legal case for harassment against Dudley." He didn't mention that the chief had practically attacked Camille the night of Thomas and Lia's wedding reception.

"Are you serious?"

He nodded. "Yeah. I'm going to have a talk with Dudley this afternoon. It's time to put a stop to this nonsense."

Thomas agreed.

As he scanned the menu, Maxwell couldn't help but glance over at Camille.

"She's looking for donations for the silent auction," Thomas told him. "It's always a huge hit at the hospital charity ball."

Maxwell smiled. "I might have something to donate."

"I thought you would," Thomas responded, a grin on his face. "I have to admit, I'm really surprised that you'd be attracted to Camille. She's nothing like the other women you've dated."

"I'm a little surprised myself," Maxwell confessed.

Chapter 5

"I hear that you are looking for donations for the silent auction," Maxwell stated as he strolled into her office.

Camille tried to keep her pleasure at seeing him from her voice. "I am," she simply said.

"Well, I'm here to give a donation," he announced.

She reached for her pen and notebook. "Are you donating your legal expertise?"

"No," Maxwell responded. "I was actually thinking of donating a cottage in Paris for a week."

Camille's eyes registered her surprise. *"Really?"*

"Yes, but please list it from an anonymous donor."

"Maxwell... Wow, thank you." She was stunned by his generosity. "No one has ever donated something so extravagant."

"I hope it brings in a lot of money."

She smiled. "I'm sure it will. This is really very generous, Maxwell."

Their gaze met and held. Neither of them spoke for a moment.

"I'm sorry," Camille murmured, breaking the silence. "Did you want something else?" She had expected him to leave her office right after his generous donation, but he was still standing there, looking at her expectantly.

"No... Actually, yes," Maxwell replied. "I wanted to let you know that I have a meeting with Dudley in about an hour."

She shifted uncomfortably in her chair. "About what happened at the reception?"

"That and some other things," he admitted. "The hospital's reputation is at stake and I'm not going to let him make matters worse."

"If you're doing this just for me, then you don't have to," she told him. "He's already apologized to me. He says that it won't happen again."

"That's good that he apologized for his bad behavior. You're a big part of why I'm talking to him, but you're not the only reason," he said cryptically.

Camille frowned. She didn't quite understand what Maxwell was saying. The thought occurred to her then that maybe someone had gone to him with a complaint against Dudley. "I'm not the only one he's..." Her voice died.

"Harassed," he finished for her. "Unfortunately no, but as I said, I'm going to put an end to it once and for all."

"Thank you," she said.

His smile sent a flash of heat that radiated throughout her body.

Camille flushed hotly at the thoughts racing around her head. It had been a while since she'd felt such emotions, but she'd never felt them as intensely as when Maxwell was around.

What am I doing? What do I have to offer a man like Maxwell Wade?

One of the qualities that attracted Maxwell to Camille was her genuine smile, which seemed prominently on display at all times. She was nothing like the women he usually dated. She wore her hair short and natural, which suited her to perfection. She didn't wear makeup and was more conservative in the way she dressed. Still, he found her incredibly sexy.

Maxwell knew that there was more to Camille and his curiosity was aroused. He wanted to know everything about her. He had to remind himself that he was only in Alexandria for a short time. It would be unwise for him to get involved with anyone.

It wasn't always easy to avoid distractions. Maxwell constantly had to deal with overly aggressive women who practically threw themselves at him. His mind traveled back to Camille.

She was nothing like that. A woman like Camille would be looking to settle down and raise a family—something he wasn't sure he was ready for.

A tremor of disappointment slid down his spine.

Dr. Dudley strode into Maxwell's office with purpose, interrupting his errant thoughts. "So what's this meeting about?" he asked.

He waited until the chief of staff took a seat before saying, "This is about you."

"Excuse me?"

"As you are aware, the hospital is in jeopardy of losing more funding and gaining more lawsuits."

Dudley's eyes shifted away from Maxwell. "What does this have to do with me?"

"Do you remember what happened at the reception?" Maxwell questioned.

"I had quite a bit to drink," Dudley responded. "I don't usually get so out of sorts, but—"

"I'm talking about Camille Hunter and how you practically attacked her."

Dudley paled. "I've apologized to her for my behavior."

Maxwell couldn't help but wonder if Dudley thought that was all he had to do to make things right. It would take more than an apology to make Camille feel comfortable in her work environment again.

"It has come to my attention that you may have a problem keeping your hands to yourself," Maxwell stated. "Don't you think it's hypocritical of you since you are the one who actually put the non-fraternization policy in place?"

"I don't know what you're talking about."

"Not only are you harassing some of the women on your staff, but you are also having an affair with one of your nurses."

Dudley's eyes grew wide as saucers and his mouth dropped open in shock. "I…I don't know what you've been told, but it's all lies."

"Don't lie to me," Maxwell warned. "I can't help you if you are not going to face up to the truth."

"What are you saying to me?" Dudley asked.

"Stop harassing your employees. If you don't, the hospital will be dealing with several sexual harassment lawsuits. As for your affair with Nurse Tsang, you have your conscience to deal with. However, if you refuse to stop harassing the female staff, then you may have your wife to deal with as well."

Dudley glared at him. "Are you threatening me?"

"It's not a threat," Maxwell said smoothly. "I'm simply stating a fact. The last thing you want is the board to get wind of what's been going on in the hospital. Rumors have a way of getting around."

"I brought you in to help us with the Matthews case."

"You brought me in to help keep the hospital from losing everything," Maxwell countered. "I'm doing what you hired me to do—protect the hospital."

Dudley sighed in resignation. "You've had your say, Maxwell. I will take everything you've said under advisement."

"See that you do," Maxwell stated.

He wasn't fazed by the angry glare Dudley bestowed on him before storming out of his office. Maxwell meant what he'd said. He was going to protect Hopewell General and its employees, even if it meant blowing the whistle on the chief of staff.

"We need to go over the silent auction items," Camille told her assistant as she opened her planner. "We have dinners, an overnight at a bed-and-breakfast for two, a private meal provided by a four-star chef, a week in a cottage in France, and—"

"Who donated that?" Lori asked.

"An anonymous donor," Camille answered. She still couldn't get over Maxwell's generosity. He had further surprised her when he had Ray drop off a check to her, adding to the extravagant donation.

"Wow. That should really bring in some nice money. We've got some really nice stuff for this year's auction."

Camille agreed. "This is just the initial response.

I still have a few more donors we are waiting to hear from, but I believe that what we have here will be our big-ticket items."

After she went over some other details of the auction with Lori, her assistant went back to her desk. As Lori left, Jerome stopped by her office.

"Have you finished your Christmas shopping?" he wanted to know.

Camille shook her head. "I've been so busy working on this charity ball that I haven't really thought much about anything else. Christmas isn't that far off, though, so I need to get started." She made a few notes before adding, "But my list isn't that long, so I should be able to get it all done in one swoop."

Jerome's pager went off. "I'm needed by Miss Thang, so I'd better get down to the O.R."

"I'll call you later."

He nodded and rushed out of her office.

Camille checked her watch. It was already past seven. Her workday ended at five, but she was in no rush to go home. She decided to continue working on her plans for the fundraiser.

Isabelle stuck her head inside the office and said, "I didn't know you were still here."

"I decided to stay late to log in the donations for the silent auction," Camille explained. "I'm surprised you're still hanging around the hospital. Didn't your shift end at seven?"

"I was hoping to run into Maxwell," Isabelle confessed. "I thought we could have dinner together, but he's in the conference room with Ray. They have been in there for almost three hours now. Ray's assistant just delivered some food to them, so I guess they plan on working really late."

"So are you and Maxwell seeing each other?" Camille couldn't resist asking.

"No," Isabelle responded. "But I'm working on it."

"I'm sure you are," Camille muttered.

"He's single and I'm single. Why shouldn't I?"

Camille met her gaze. "No reason, Isabelle."

Isabelle sat down beside her on the sofa. "Hey, are you interested in Maxwell?"

"Why would you ask me something like that?"

"You've been acting weird around me since you saw us in his office." Isabelle tossed her hair over her shoulder. "I don't know, but I get the feeling that seeing Maxwell with me bothered you."

"Isabelle, you're mistaken," Camille responded quickly.

"I'm relieved to hear that."

Camille wanted to ask Isabelle why, but she remained quiet. She knew her friend well enough to know that she was on a fact-finding mission. She had come to see if Camille was interested in Maxwell.

"Well, I don't know about you, but I'm exhausted," Isabelle stated. "I'm going home. I'll have to ask Maxwell out another night."

"Have you considered letting him ask you out?" Camille inquired. "He may be old-fashioned when it comes to stuff like this."

"Or he might be flattered that I'm making the first move," Isabelle countered.

"Well, it's really up to you," Camille told her. "Have a good evening and I'll see you tomorrow."

"How much longer do you plan on staying?" Isabelle asked, pausing in the doorway.

"Just long enough to finish this log."

"Need any help?" Isabelle offered.

Camille shook her head. "Thanks, but I have everything under control."

If only that were really true, she thought silently. She knew that Isabelle wasn't really interested in helping her. She was simply trying to find a reason to stay at the hospital in the hopes of seeing Maxwell.

Isabelle gave up and decided to leave.

An hour had passed when Camille was startled at the unexpected knock on her open door.

"I didn't mean to scare you," Maxwell told her. "I saw that you were still here so I wanted to give you an update on my meeting with Dr. Dudley."

"How did it go?"

He leaned against the door. "Okay, I think. You shouldn't have any more problems with him."

She sighed in relief. "That's great news. He did apologize to me and I believe he was sincere, but...I don't know if I'll ever feel comfortable around him."

"It may take some time, but just make sure he doesn't cross any professional boundaries with you," Maxwell advised.

Camille nodded in understanding. "Thank you for everything you've done."

She stood. "It's late so I should get going. I have to be here early tomorrow morning."

Deep down she really didn't want to leave because enjoyed herself whenever Maxwell was around. He had a special way of making her feel safe.

"I'll see you tomorrow then."

Camille gave him a smile. "Yes, you will."

"I was on my way out, so I'll walk you to your car."

She was secretly thrilled.

Chapter 6

The next day, Maxwell leaned back in the leather desk chair. He couldn't stop thinking about Camille. She had dominated his thoughts most of last night and again this morning.

He had just accepted the email meeting invitation she'd sent him for the following day, but he didn't want to wait that long to see her again.

He pushed away from the desk and rose to his full height.

Maxwell left his office and walked around the corner to where Camille's office was located. She was on the telephone when he arrived.

He stood in the doorway until she gestured for him to come inside and sit down.

"I'll give you a call later this afternoon," she told the person on the other end of the line. "Great. That's what I want to hear."

Camille gave him an apologetic smile, and then said, "I'll call you about one-thirty. We can finish up then. Goodbye."

She hung up the phone. "Sorry about that."

"No need to apologize," Maxwell told her. "I'm the one interrupting. I know we're scheduled for a meeting tomorrow, but I'd like to take you to lunch today."

Camille smiled at him. "I was about to have lunch, so sure. I'd love to take you up on your invitation. If you want, we can cancel the meeting for tomorrow and just do it while we're eating."

Maxwell shook his head. "No, this is just lunch. No discussion of business."

"Oh, okay." She stood up, reached for her purse and grabbed her coat.

He knew that he could have asked any of the single women working in the hospital to have lunch with him, but it was Camille's company that he desired. Maxwell wasn't sure why he felt so drawn to her.

"Where are we going?" Camille inquired.

He smiled at her and said, "I'm open to suggestions."

"Do you trust me?"

Maxwell nodded. "I do."

"I know just the place," she told him. "It's about three blocks from here."

"I'll drive."

Camille was aware of everyone staring as they made their way to the hospital exit. The rumor mill was going to busy this afternoon for sure.

Maxwell opened the passenger door for Camille before he got in.

He had never been to the restaurant she picked, but was looking forward to enjoying a nice lunch with a beautiful woman.

A few minutes later, Maxwell escorted her into the restaurant where the delicious scent of freshly sautéed garlic and herbs tantalized their senses.

A smiling hostess greeted them warmly.

They were quickly seated at an intimate corner table in the main dining room. The mustard-gold walls and deep-emerald-colored drapes provided a richly colored backdrop while soft music floated throughout the restaurant.

"Do you come here often?" Maxwell asked her.

Camille shook her head. "Not as much as I'd like. I don't really enjoy eating alone."

He wanted to ask if she was seeing someone, but Maxwell decided that it was much too soon for such personal questions.

He perused the menu while they waited for a member of the waitstaff to arrive. "Everything on here sounds delicious."

"I've tried almost every entrée," Camille stated. "All of them have been delicious. I don't think you can go wrong with whatever you choose." She was extremely conscious of his virile appeal.

The waitress arrived to take their drink order. They gave her their lunch selections as well.

Camille met Maxwell's gaze with a smile. "Thanks for lunch."

He chuckled. "We haven't eaten yet."

"I know, but it's never too soon to say thank you. This is so much nicer than having an egg salad sandwich in my office."

"You don't go out for lunch?"

"Only if I'm having lunch with someone," she responded.

The waitress returned with their drinks.

Maxwell took a long sip of his iced tea. "Camille, I want you to know that what you saw between me and Isabelle was not what you thought."

"So you're saying that I didn't really see her in your arms," she replied. "And I didn't see you were holding her very closely. That's what you're trying to tell me, right?"

Maxwell shook his head. "It was nothing like that at all. She tripped over something and I grabbed her to keep her from falling. It was completely innocent."

Camille couldn't help but wonder if Isabelle had staged her fall purposely to end up in Maxwell's arms. She kept her suspicions to herself.

"The hospital has its share of scandals," she began. "Something like that would've kept the staff talking for days."

"Are you worried that I'll be compromised?" Maxwell interjected. "I'm touched that you care."

Heat rushed to Camille's face. "I just think that you should be careful. That's all."

The waitress arrived with their orders and Maxwell blessed the food before they dived in to sample their meals.

"So what do you think?" Camille asked after Maxwell tried his chicken.

He wiped his mouth on his napkin. "It's great."

She took a sip of her lemonade. "I told you that it was delicious."

"Tell me something, Camille. What do you do when you're not the PR whiz at Hopewell General?"

"I play basketball," she responded. "During the summer, I teach water aerobics."

"I'm impressed," Maxwell said. "I had a feeling that there was a lot more to you than meets the eye."

"I'm sure I could say the same about you." Camille inclined her head and said, "Tell me something that most people wouldn't know about you."

He thought for a moment, and then replied, "I love to cook. Most people wouldn't know that about me."

She broke into a grin. "Wow, I would have never thought that about you. What a nice surprise."

"It's your turn," Maxwell stated. "Tell me something about yourself that most people don't know."

"Most people don't know that I love motorcycles. Sometimes I ride during the summer."

He couldn't hide his shock. "*Really?* You actually ride a motorcycle?"

Camille nodded. "With Jerome—he's my best friend. We both own bikes and we ride together some time."

Maxwell was speechless. "I... Wow...that's something I've always wanted to do. Ride a motorcycle."

"You should," Camille encouraged. "It's a lot of fun."

Maxwell enjoyed this peek into the adventurous side of Camille.

Their gaze met and held, making Camille nervous. She thought she detected a flicker in his intense eyes, causing her pulse to skitter alarmingly.

Maxwell pointed toward her plate. "You're not eating."

She grinned. "I'm not as hungry as I thought. I'm going to take it back with me. I'll eat it later." Camille never tired of looking at him.

Maxwell took another bite of his chicken. "This is really delicious. I'm glad you chose this place. Now that I know about it—I'll come back here often."

"I'm glad you like it." Camille finished off her glass of lemonade. "What do you like to do when you're not working, Maxwell?"

"I enjoy basketball as well," he responded. "Dancing is a favorite pastime and so is reading."

"We have a lot in common," Camille said.

"You seemed a little surprised by that."

"I guess I am," she confessed. "When I look at you... well, I just assumed that we wouldn't share the same interests. I suppose what they say about assumptions is correct."

He chuckled. "If it makes you feel any better, I didn't think we'd have anything in common, either."

After the waitress dropped off the check, Maxwell reached inside his wallet and pulled out two twenty-dollar bills. He dropped them on the table and rose to his feet.

"I guess we should head back to the hospital."

"I'm afraid tongues are probably wagging."

He shrugged. "I don't care. We are working together and there's nothing wrong with two coworkers having lunch together."

Camille agreed, but she knew how some people liked to gossip. She also didn't want any drama with Isabelle. But then again it wasn't like Isabelle and Maxwell were dating.

They left the restaurant and headed to the car.

"This was nice," Camille said. "I enjoyed having lunch with you."

"Same here," Maxwell responded. "We'll have to do it again sometime."

She smiled. "Sure."

As soon as they arrived back at the hospital and went their separate ways, Camille encountered Jerome. Actually he stood directly in her path.

"Hey, I heard that you and Maxwell had lunch together."

"That sure didn't take long," she muttered.

"It's true?" he asked.

"Jerome, keep your voice down, please." Camille glanced over her shoulder to where a couple of nurses were gathered. They were trying not to look as if they were listening, but she knew better.

"Let's take a walk," she told him.

"Okay, spill."

"Maxwell and I had lunch together and that's all there is to it. *We had lunch.*"

"I knew it," Jerome stated. "I knew that man had the hots for you."

"He does not," Camille responded. "We are working together. You of all people know that."

"I'm telling you...Maxwell Wade is interested in you."

"Jerome, he lives in New York. He's only here to help with the lawsuit. When it's done, he is going back home. I'm not about to get involved in a short-term relationship or a long-distance one. It doesn't work for me."

Jerome's pager went off. "I need to get to the O.R."

Camille watched him rush off as she waited for the elevator to arrive. She was joined by Jaclyn. "How's your day going?" she asked the intern.

"It was going well until my last patient. He is on a ventilator and his family is fighting over whether or not to take him off. His wife wants to keep him on it, but his children insist that their father would not want to live this way."

"Did he sign a DNR?" Camille inquired.

Jaclyn shook her head. "There's not one in his records." Lowering her voice, she added, "He was one of Terrence's patients. His kids are claiming that their father signed a DNR."

Camille released a short sigh. "This isn't good."

"His wife keeps insisting that her husband never signed the DNR form," Jaclyn stated. "I'm afraid this may end up in court."

"The patient and his family don't need to go through something like that. The hospital doesn't need it, either. However, it could be used as a strike against Terrence." Camille shook her head sadly. "This is just so messed up."

Jaclyn agreed.

"Keep me posted on his condition," Camille told her. "I want to be forewarned in the event I have to prepare a statement."

She was heavy in thought when she stepped off the elevator on the second floor. Camille paused outside of Maxwell's office when she heard Isabelle's laughter.

That woman just didn't give up.

She could hear Isabelle bragging about her cooking and offering to cook dinner for Maxwell. Camille couldn't hear his response. She felt guilty for eavesdropping.

No man was worth all this, she decided.

Camille was just about to leave the office for the day when Maxwell again appeared in her doorway.

"Maxwell, I wasn't expecting you," she said. "Do you need something?"

"I was thinking about what you said earlier and I don't like eating alone, either. Would you be interested in having dinner with me tonight?"

She thought about the way Isabelle practically threw herself at him earlier and said, "Maybe you should ask Isabelle."

Maxwell gaze was intense. "But you're the one I want to have dinner with, Camille."

She blushed, realizing how catty she sounded. "I'm sorry. I really shouldn't have said that."

He shrugged. "Isabelle is a sweet girl, but I'm just not interested in her. I would actually like to get to know you better."

Camille swallowed her surprise.

"If I'm out of line, please tell me," Maxwell said. "I don't want to make you uncomfortable."

"No, you're fine," she said quickly. "I'm just a little surprised. Maxwell, is this a date?"

He laughed. "Yes, it is."

"I guess you can tell that it's been a while since I've been on one, huh?"

"I'll pick you up at seven," Maxwell told her. "Provided you give me your address and phone number."

Camille wrote down her information.

When he left her office, she sank down in her chair. *I'm actually going on a date with Maxwell Wade. This is the last thing I ever expected.* Camille experienced a rush of excitement at the thought.

Chapter 7

Camille agreed to go out with him, which pleased Maxwell more than he ever expected. He supposed it was because she was different from any other woman he had dated in the past.

Humming softly to the music, he went over a stack of motions. Maxwell preferred staying busy. It helped to pass the time. He was looking forward to getting his day over with so that he could concentrate on Camille.

He had to find out why she fascinated him so much. He was physically attracted to Camille, as he'd been to many women. But this felt different. He was not interested in adding another notch to his bedpost. What he felt for Camille went beyond that and defied definition.

"What's got you so deep in thought?" Ray asked from the doorway.

Maxwell looked up. "I need your help with something."

Ray walked all the way into the office. "What is it?"

"I'm taking Camille out to dinner tonight. Any recommendations?"

"Bastille," Ray suggested. "The restaurant is one of the top eateries in this area. It has a variety of dishes, including seafood."

"It's French, right?"

Ray nodded.

Maxwell smiled. "Great." He had discovered during lunch that he and Camille both shared a love for French cuisine.

"I'm telling you that everything on the menu is delicious," Ray told him. "But two of my personal favorites are the red wine–braised Virginia beef and the monkfish filet. I'll have Angie make the reservations for you. What time are you picking her up?"

"Seven o'clock."

Maxwell checked his watch when Ray left the office. He was looking forward to the evening. It had been a long time since he had felt such anticipation.

Camille moved around her bedroom in a panic. *Why did I agree to go out with Maxwell? I have no idea what to wear.*

There was only one thing she could do. She picked up the phone.

"Jerome, I really need your help," she said once her friend answered. "Maxwell asked me to have dinner with him tonight and I don't know what to wear."

"What about that leather outfit I bought you for your birthday last year? I'm sure it's hanging in the closet with the tags still on it."

"I can't wear something like that, Jerome. If I was

a dominatrix or something, then it wouldn't be a problem."

He laughed. "Whip me, mommy. I've been a bad boy."

She didn't find the humor in it. "Focus, Jerome. I really need your help."

"Okay, so what time is your date?"

Camille glanced over at the clock. "In a couple of hours."

"I'll be there in about ten minutes."

"Jerome, thanks so much." The relief in her voice was audible. "I appreciate your help."

She hung up the phone and sat down to wait for Jerome to arrive. Thoughts of Maxwell besieged her. Why was she so nervous about this date? Why did he affect her the way she did?

Before she came up with any answers, Jerome showed up.

"Help has arrived," Jerome announced, walking briskly through the door. "Camille, you know I love you, but we need to find you a girlfriend to help you with fashion emergencies."

"Jerome, the reason I asked you is because you are a man. I want to look nice for my dinner with Maxwell. He's used to spending time with models and actresses. You know that I've always been more of a tomboy."

"So what's going on between you and Mr. Wade?" he inquired. "You had lunch with him earlier and now you two are having dinner together?"

"I don't know," she admitted. "He asked me on a date, so I guess we're just seeing where this takes us."

"You know the hospital grapevine was busy today," he told her. "Isabelle almost fell out of her chair when she heard that you were having lunch with Maxwell."

"I'm surprised you all ever get any work done with all of the gossiping going on."

"Hey, I don't gossip—I just listen."

"I guess Isabelle's not going to be too happy with me," Camille murmured. "She was really on a mission where Maxwell is concerned."

"Well, he decided he wanted you, so Isabelle will just have to get over herself." Jerome gestured toward the closet. "Pick out your most daring outfits. Let me see what we can come up with."

Camille pulled out a bright red dress with ruffles.

Jerome threw back his head laughing.

"What?" she asked. "You said daring. Well, I'd have to be daring if I wore this thing anywhere."

"Where did you get that from?"

"My mother sent this to me." Camille laughed. "She still thinks I'm her little girl."

"Throw that thing in the trash."

Camille tossed it on the bed, and then walked back into her closet. This time she came out with a purple long-sleeved dress with a black leather belt. She didn't really own anything daring.

Jerome shook his head. "Try again."

She tossed that one on the bed. "Maybe I should just cancel."

"I didn't hear that," Jerome told her. "I know you have something in that huge closet of yours."

"What about this?"

Camille held up a black jersey knit dress with a silver-and-black belt. If this outfit didn't make the cut, then she was going to call Maxwell and ask for a rain check. She made a mental note to plan a day of shopping just to refresh her wardrobe.

"That's the one. It hugs your body just right," Jerome stated. "Wear your black leather boots. The ones with the silver studs. No man can resist them."

She smiled. "Thanks, Jerome."

"Are you planning on wearing any makeup?"

Camille frowned. "Do I need to?"

"Just a little," he suggested. "Just to enhance your natural beauty."

Jerome sat in the living room watching television while Camille showered and prepared for her date.

When she descended the stairs, he whistled. "You look gorgeous."

Camille dismissed his words with a wave of her hand. "Be serious."

"I am," Jerome responded.

She sank down beside him. "What am I doing? Even with this outfit and makeup on, I am no match for a man like Maxwell."

"I believe he would disagree with you, Camille."

"He dates supermodels, Jerome. I can barely put on eyeliner."

Jerome embraced her. "Just be yourself."

Camille nodded in agreement. "You're right. I only know how to be me, so I might as well make the most of the evening."

Jerome continued his pep talk until he left, fifteen minutes before Maxwell was due to arrive.

Camille surveyed her reflection in the mirror once more. She was pleased with what she saw, but would Maxwell be disappointed?

Shaking off her insecurities, Camille resolved to have a nice evening with him with no expectations of anything more. This way she didn't have to worry about being disappointed.

* * *

"Have you eaten here before?" Maxwell asked.

Camille nodded. "I've only been here a couple of times. The food is really great."

"If the food is so great, why have you only come here a couple of times to eat?" Maxwell inquired.

She smiled. "Look around you. It's more of a couples-type restaurant. Usually if I decide to eat out, I'll call ahead and pick up my dinner."

"See, we actually have something else in common."

Grinning, Camille responded, "Imagine that."

"Tell me something," Maxwell began. "Why did you suggest that I have dinner with Isabelle when I asked you out? Is it because she was waiting for me in my office when we returned from lunch?"

"She's made it pretty obvious that she's into you."

Maxwell nodded in agreement. "She has, but relationships only work when two people are involved. Isabelle is quite beautiful, but I am attracted to you."

His bluntness caught her off guard.

Their eyes locked as their breathing seemed to come in unison.

After a moment, Camille decided it was time for her to be honest with Maxwell. "I'm attracted to you as well."

He visibly relaxed.

The waiter's appearance put a temporary block on their conversation. He served Maxwell and Camille the first course of New England rock shrimp beignets.

Camille took a bite and closed her eyes, savoring the flavor. "This is so good."

Maxwell agreed.

Just before they finished the beignets, the second course arrived.

He reached over and took Camille's hand. "I've wanted to do this all evening."

A delicious shudder heated her body at his touch. Camille felt the heat of desire wash over her like waves. Her eyes traveled to his lips. She wanted so much to feel the touch of his mouth against hers. She cleared her throat, pretending not to be affected by him or his touch. Instead, she sampled the goat cheese terrine and frisée-apple.

"What's wrong?" he asked her, pointing at her plate. "You don't like it?"

"I'm trying to make sure I have room for the rest of my meal."

He smiled in response, his eyes never leaving her face.

"You're staring," Camille murmured.

"I find you incredibly beautiful."

"Thank you for the compliment," she said. "You're very sweet." Her senses reeled as if short-circuited and made her knees tremble. Good thing she was sitting, or she feared they wouldn't hold her up.

From the moment she'd opened her door to Maxwell at her town house, he had openly admired the way she looked for their date. He had complimented her at least twice on her dress and her hair. Camille noted how handsome Maxwell looked in the gray suit he was wearing. She was totally entranced by his compelling personage.

For their third course, she dined on monkfish while Matthew had chosen the Moulard duck breast with Calvados-cider sauce.

Camille used the corner of her napkin to wipe her mouth. "Have you ever been here before?"

Shaking his head, Maxwell responded, "This is my first time."

"Oh, so how did you know about Bastille?"

"I asked Ray for a recommendation."

She gave him a sidelong glance. "Maxwell, can I ask you a question?"

He met her gaze. "Sure."

"Do you ever just relax?" she asked.

Stroking his chin, Maxwell regarded her carefully. "Believe it or not, I actually know how to have a good time."

"What constitutes a good time to you?" Camille questioned with a grin. "What is it that you do for fun?"

Maxwell leaned forward, gazing into her eyes. "Do you really want to know what I enjoy doing for pleasure?"

Camille flushed hotly.

Maxwell broke into laughter. "Besides cooking, I also enjoy reading mysteries. I also like going to art museums, exhibits…stuff like that. What do you do for fun?"

"I love the water so I like spending a lot of time on a beach during the summer," Camille responded. "I'm also a huge history buff—I'm always taking tours. And of course, I love music."

"Interesting…" The warmth of his smile echoed in his voice. "I love history myself."

"There are several contemporary art exhibits there right now, but they're only going to be here for a couple of weeks. Would you like to see them?"

Maxwell held her gaze. "I'd love to," he responded.

His eyes shimmered with the light from the window, and the smile he gave her sent her pulse racing.

After their dinner, neither one of them wanted to end the evening, so they went back to her place.

Camille made a pot of coffee, and then sat down with Maxwell in the living room.

"You're nothing like the man I thought you were," she confessed.

He chuckled. "Do I even want to know?"

She shook her head.

Maxwell reached over, pulling her closer to him. He seemed to read her thoughts because he took her in his arms and kissed her passionately.

When Maxwell pulled away, he said, "I've really wanted to do that since the moment we got here."

In response, Camille pulled his head down to hers. Their lips met again and she felt buffeted by the winds of a savage harmony. Her senses reeled as if short-circuited and made her knees tremble.

Breaking their kiss, she buried her face against his throat; her trembling limbs clung to him helplessly. She was extremely conscious of where his warm flesh touched hers.

Maxwell touched a finger to her chin, lifting her face to his view. His eyes were bright with an emotion she had not often seen but could identify.

Lust.

From his expression, Camille knew her own eyes reflected the same.

His mouth curved up at the corners. His finger brushed against her skin, moving back and forth, making it difficult to think.

Desire ignited in her belly, causing her to pull away reluctantly. She didn't want Maxwell to think that she was easy.

"What's wrong, sweetheart?"

"Nothing. I just don't think it's a good idea for us to get carried away," she murmured.

Her gaze locked with his and she could see her passion mirrored in his eyes. She was so swept up in the moment that when Maxwell pulled her back into his arms, she could not refuse. He kissed her again, lingering, savoring every moment. Camille's emotions whirled. Blood pounded in her brain, leapt from her heart and made her knees tremble.

"I have always been drawn to you, sweetheart," Maxwell said. "From the moment I laid eyes on you." He touched his lips to hers again.

Camille kissed him with a hunger that belied her outward calm. She was consumed by him, powerless to resist him. Shocked by her own eager response, she realized resisting Maxwell was the last thing on her mind.

Chapter 8

Maxwell couldn't believe it.

He'd had Camille in his arms, all soft and willing, and he'd walked away. He didn't want to leave Camille's townhome, but he could tell that she wasn't ready for them to become intimate. Although his body told him otherwise, Maxwell thought it was too soon as well. He wasn't expecting a one-night stand—just a nice dinner with a beautiful woman and pleasant conversation. Recalling the feel of Camille's lips against his, Maxwell decided he'd gotten much more.

When he entered his hotel room he undressed and immediately jumped into the shower. He needed one. A cold one. Something to cool his ardor.

After slipping on a pair of pajama bottoms and a T-shirt, he settled down on the sofa and turned on the television.

Kendra stepping out of a sleek, black limo amidst

of a sea of hungry photographers and reporters stilled his hand.

Maxwell had never watched her reality show and was about to change the channel until he heard her mention his name. He turned the volume up.

"I just got off the phone with Maxwell," she was telling her BFF, Candy, who was also on the show. "I told him that I was getting tired of waiting on him to pop the question. I'm ready to get married and have a baby."

He frowned. They had never had that discussion. Maxwell had brought up the subject of marriage only once and that was almost six years ago. Kendra had refused him. At the time he was disappointed, but now he was relieved. A marriage between the two of them would surely have ended in divorce.

Maxwell hated how she enjoyed bringing up his name on her reality series. The show was in its second season and wildly popular. Apparently viewers enjoyed the antics of Kendra and her supermodel gal pals.

His mouth tightened as Kendra began discussing his sexual prowess in bed. "Shut up," he whispered.

Grinning, Kendra was posing for more photos along the red carpet. The camera crew followed her as she attended some Hollywood premiere.

Maxwell turned off the television.

He was not going to let Kendra ruin what had been a pleasant evening. Instead, he went to bed, settling back against the pillows and letting his thoughts wander to Camille.

What he was feeling for her was more than infatuation. It was a desire that burned like embers inside him. In the short time that they'd spent getting to know one another, he knew his attraction to her was more than just a fleeting passion. It was a fondness, a kinship.

It defied an explanation.

Camille's lips were still tender from Maxwell's passion-filled kisses. Her body temperature hadn't cooled yet, so she decided to take a bubble bath, hoping to ease some of the pent-up tension she felt.

No man had ever made her feel the way Maxwell made her feel. His experienced touch left her burning with desire.

Camille was still a virgin.

She had seen what happened to her friends who had decided to jump into physical relationships that eventually ended badly. Camille was determined that she would remain celibate until the right man came along.

The way Maxwell had been able to stir her emotions, she wondered if he was the one for her.

Don't get ahead of yourself, she cautioned her heart.

Camille didn't want to set herself up for heartbreak. Besides, she didn't know how he would respond once he found out that she was inexperienced.

What if he was turned off? After all, he was used to more sophisticated and experienced women.

Suddenly chilled, she got out of the bath and slipped on a pair of old sweats and a sweatshirt. She crawled into bed and turned on the television. As if to taunt her, Kendra's reality show came on. Camille watched it, until the model began talking about how good Maxwell was in bed.

Then she changed the channel.

"I'd rather find out for myself," she whispered to no one but herself.

An image of Maxwell formed in her mind, bringing

a smile to her lips. He was all she thought about until she fell asleep.

When next Camille opened her eyes, she sat up in bed and glanced over at the clock. It was five minutes after six—almost time for her to get up. She shut down the alarm clock to keep it from going off, and then eased out of bed.

She had spent most of the night dreaming about Maxwell.

Strange, she thought, how a man could dominate her waking and sleeping hours as he did. As she brushed her teeth, realization dawned on her.

I'm falling in love with Maxwell.

Her heart skipped a beat at the mere thought of his name. Camille prayed that she wasn't getting too ahead of herself.

I'm just going to enjoy the time I have with Maxwell. She didn't want to forget that he would be returning to New York once the lawsuit was over.

The thought saddened her, but it was a fact she could not ignore.

Maxwell's day brightened the moment he saw Camille in the hospital lobby. She had been on his mind since last night. He wanted to kiss her, but since they were in the hospital, they had to maintain professional boundaries.

"Good morning," she greeted.

"Good morning," he said in return. Lowering his voice, he whispered, "I enjoyed our evening last night."

She broke into a grin. "So did I."

Dr. Dudley spied them as he walked in and paused, as if looking for a way to avoid them. With no escape route in sight, he walked up to them. "Good morning."

He eyed Maxwell a moment before turning to Camille. "I trust everything is going well with the planning of the hospital fundraiser."

"It is," she confirmed. "Everything is also set for the Christmas party for the pediatric wing. Will you be playing Santa Claus again this year?"

Over the last few days Dr. Dudley had kept his word and his distance, but there was still an air of tension that existed between them. She could feel it now.

He nodded. "I have the suit all pressed and ready."

She gave him a tiny smile. "It sounds great."

When a team of surgeons entered the front door, Dr. Dudley excused himself and continued down the hallway with them.

"I don't think he likes you much," Camille observed aloud.

"He doesn't," Maxwell confirmed with a shrug. "But I'm okay with that."

They took the elevator to the second floor.

Isabelle was standing outside of Maxwell's office. Her eyes registered her shock when she saw the two of them get off the elevator together.

"Good morning, Isabelle," Camille said quietly. She could feel the tension in the air.

Before Isabelle could respond, Maxwell asked, "Did you need something?"

"Actually, no," she answered. "I came up here to see Angie, but she's not at her desk. I thought maybe she was the one getting off the elevator."

Camille could tell that Isabelle was lying. She had come up to see Maxwell, but was too embarrassed now to admit it.

She turned to Maxwell and said, "I'll talk to you later."

He nodded. "I'd like to meet with you at some point to discuss the suit."

Camille stole a glance at Isabelle and said, "Send me an email with a list of times you're available."

She rushed off to her office.

A few minutes later, Isabelle showed up in her doorway. "Do you have a moment?" she asked.

Camille took a deep breath and exhaled slowly. "Sure. What is it?"

"Are you going out with Maxwell?"

"Not that it's any of your business, but we had dinner last night."

"And lunch yesterday," Isabelle interjected. "Sounds to me like you two are an item."

"I don't know if I would go that far," Camille responded. The truth was that she didn't know exactly how to define their relationship. It was much too soon to tell.

"You knew that I was interested in him."

"I didn't go after Maxwell, if that's what you're thinking, Isabelle. I would think that you'd know me better than that."

After a moment, during which numerous emotions showed on Isabelle's face, she nodded her head. "I know that. It's just hard to accept that Maxwell Wade didn't want me. I need some time, but I'll get over it." She awarded Camille a huge smile. "Congrats, girl."

Camille didn't like seeing her friend so upset. "I wouldn't do anything to hurt you, Isabelle."

"I know. Hey, it's not like I ever dated the man. He wouldn't even give me a chance."

Her pager went off.

"Oh, I need to go. My patient is coding." Isabelle rushed off.

Camille released a small sigh of relief. She didn't want anything, including Maxwell, to come between her and Isabelle.

When she checked her email, she found that Maxwell had already requested to meet with her at eleven. Camille checked her schedule, and then replied that she was free at that time.

She thought about Jaclyn and the patient they had discussed. Camille got up from her desk and went looking for her friend. She wanted to find out how things were going with the family.

Camille found Jaclyn working on some paperwork at the nurse's station on the fourth floor.

"Hey, how is your patient?" she asked.

"He's still on the ventilator," Jaclyn replied. "Mrs. Waterford never leaves his side. I think she's afraid that one of the children will pull the plug on her husband. She has given strict orders that they are not supposed to be alone with him."

"What does Dr. Dudley say?"

"We can't do anything without the DNR," Jaclyn stated. "Mrs. Waterford is the patient's wife and we have to abide by her wishes."

A woman walked to the doorway of the hospital room across from the nurse's station. "Dr. Campbell, come quick," she said. "The patient just moved his fingers."

'I'll talk to you later," Camille told her.

When Jaclyn went to check on her patient, one of the nurses said, "It's a shame the way those kids are acting. They were arguing so loudly last night that Mrs. Waterford had security come and escort them out of the hospital."

The situation certainly was sad, but all Camille could

do was be there for her friend. Right now she had work to do.

Back in her office, she made several phone calls to follow up with the holiday fundraiser. She checked in with the vendors, she confirmed the menu with the hotel, and she ordered the Christmas tree for the hospital.

Camille met with her staff to get updates on current projects. Afterward, she sat down to prepare for her meeting with Maxwell.

He arrived promptly at eleven.

"How has your morning been?" he asked her.

"Busy," Camille replied. "How about yours?"

"Same." Maxwell sat down in one of the visitor chairs. "Now, about the Matthews case…I'm meeting with his attorney later in the week. I'm hoping we can get something settled quickly."

"That would be nice," she responded. "I'd like to shift the focus off of the lawsuit and onto the charity ball and the annual children's Christmas party."

As she spoke she noticed Maxwell's eyes travel from her eyes to her lips.

She felt her temperature rise and shifted nervously in her chair. "We…" She shook her head, and then tried again. "I'm sorry. I lost my train of thought."

He laughed.

"I can't believe that you're having this effect on me."

"I glad that I'm not the only one who can't concentrate."

She met his gaze. "What are we doing, Maxwell?"

"Getting to know one another," he said smoothly. "We are exploring where this is going to take us."

"I needed to hear that," she told him. "I wanted to make sure we're on the same page."

Maxwell reached across the table and covered her hand with his. "We are."

Camille smiled. She wished they were anywhere but at the hospital, where they had to maintain an appropriate facade. But since they were, she forced herself to get it together and returned her attention to the reason for their meeting.

She listened closely while Maxwell detailed the legal implications of the scandals plaguing the hospital, and then went on to discuss the work Thomas's wife, Lia, had done for the hospital.

When Lia's son was ill, she was determined to learn the identity of the sperm donor who fathered her child, even when it meant breaking the law by hacking into the hospital's database. It turned out that Grady Bradshaw was the father. He donated bone marrow to save his son, and fell in love with Lia. After their wedding, the FBI systems analyst was hired to keep other hackers from accessing medical files and other personal information. She created and installed impenetrable security systems.

"Why don't I send out a press release detailing the state-of-the-art protocols?" Camille suggested. "I could also launch an awareness campaign on the issue. We can improve Hopewell's image in this area at least."

Despite her earlier resolve, it was a struggle for Camille to keep her attention on business. She hungered for the touch of his lips against hers. It was as if she was addicted to his kisses. It was an addiction she did not want to give up.

But there was one more case she needed to bring up with Maxwell.

"We have a right-to-die issue that might actually end up in court," she told him. "The patient is in a coma and his children want to pull the plug, but his wife—their stepmother—wants to keep him alive."

"I take it the kids stand to inherit all of his wealth when he dies."

She nodded. "That's my understanding."

"Is there a living will or advance directive on file?"

"We don't have one on file. His children are adamant that he would not want to remain on life support, but his wife disagrees." She shook her head. "And there's one more problem. Terrence Matthews was the patient's doctor."

"Do the kids think that he signed one and it's been misplaced?" Maxwell asked.

"I don't know, but it could come up."

He gave a slight shrug. "If no signed DNR is on file or was handed to medical personnel, then the hospital has to do everything possible to save the patient's life."

"It's really sad to see the family fighting over something like this," Camille murmured. "This is a time when they really need each other."

Maxwell nodded in agreement. "I'll do some research on my end on this type of case. It's best to be prepared."

Camille couldn't agree more.

Maxwell left Camille's office and went to see the chief of staff.

It was clear that Dr. Dudley wasn't pleased to see him. His whole demeanor changed when Maxwell strode into his prestigious corner office.

"What can I do to help you, Maxwell?"

Maxwell wasted no time with formalities and small talk. "I think you should consider drafting new wording on the 'no fraternizing' policy."

"Why are you so interested? Is it because of Camille?"

"I don't work for you, so your policy doesn't affect me," Maxwell responded. "With a policy like this in place, you force your staff to keep secrets. They work long hours together, and it's natural with as much time as they spend together that people fall in love. If you don't change things, the current policy will increasingly become a problem."

Dudley's eyes revealed his frustration, but Maxwell didn't back down. He continued to argue his point.

He did not leave Dudley's office until the man agreed to consider his suggestion. Satisfied, Maxwell went back to his office where he recounted his conversation with the chief to Ray.

"I'm pretty sure Dudley will be thrilled when I return to New York," Maxwell stated.

Ray laughed. "You're probably right."

Maxwell finished his work day and headed to the hotel. He had hoped to spend time with Camille, but she was meeting with the event coordinator to go over some items for the charity ball.

He changed into a pair of sweats and settled down on the sofa with a stack of case files and a sandwich from room service.

While he worked and ate, Maxwell's thoughts skittered to Camille. She was such a sweet and caring woman, she deserved a man who would treat her like a queen. Was he that man?

Maxwell knew that Camille had gotten under his skin. But what would happen between them when he returned to New York?

He would never consider living in Alexandria. It was completely out of the question. Before they became too involved, Maxwell wanted to find out how Camille felt about long-distance relationships.

I really don't want to lose her.

The thought came out of nowhere, shaking Maxwell to the core.

Chapter 9

"I missed you last night," Maxwell said when Camille strolled into his office. She looked beautiful in the gray pinstripe suit she was wearing.

She smiled. "I missed you, too. I thought about calling you, but it was late when I got home."

"I was probably up," he told her.

"Well, I was thinking that maybe I could cook dinner for you tonight," she told him. "If you're not busy."

He broke into a grin. "I would love a real home-cooked meal."

Camille folded her arms across her chest. "I hope that I don't disappoint you then."

"You won't," he reassured her.

Camille left Maxwell's office and strolled around the corner to hers. She spent a few minutes going over her calendar with her assistant before sitting down at her desk to work on a press release.

When that was done she pulled out her Christmas shopping list and added Maxwell's name to it.

"What do you buy the man who has everything?" she whispered. Camille made a mental note to ask Jerome to help her find something nice for Maxwell.

As she mentally listed some suggestions, she spotted Jaclyn in the hallway and called out her name.

"How is your patient doing?" she asked. "The one in the coma."

"Oh, Robert Waterford. Nothing's changed."

"What happened to him?" Camille inquired.

"He was hit by another driver and lost control of his car," Jaclyn said. "When the paramedics arrived, they were able to restore his breathing and heartbeat and he was transported, unconscious, to hospital."

"He's been in a coma since the accident?" Camille asked.

Jaclyn nodded. "I keep hoping for a Christmas miracle."

"Have faith."

They talked for a few minutes more, and then Jaclyn left to meet Lucien. They were making plans for their wedding.

Camille recalled a case where a female patient had suffered contraction of her four extremities with irreversible muscle and tendon damage. The patient had no cognitive or reflex ability to swallow food or water and would never recover such ability. The husband and her family were at odds because he told the doctors that his wife would not wish to continue her life unless she could have a normal life. Her family disagreed, so they ended up in court. After a couple of years, a court found that, although her respiration and circulation continued unaided, she was oblivious to her surroundings and her brain had degenerated. She hated to see the Waterfords endure such a protracted legal battle.

The Waterford family was another prominent family in Alexandria, so any legal action on the part of the family would end up as front-page news.

The Waterfords had donated quite a bit of money to the hospital as well, although not as much as the Matthews family. Camille shook her head. The hospital couldn't afford to lose any more donors.

She raised her eyes heavenward and whispered, "We really do need a miracle."

Camille eyed the dining room table and smiled. She had scented candles stationed around the room and in the center of the table. She had rushed home after work to cook and get ready for her dinner date with Maxwell.

I want this evening to be perfect.

Humming softly, Camille strolled into the kitchen to see how her meal was faring. Her chicken had been in the slow cooker since she left for work on a low temperature. She opened the oven to check on the scalloped potatoes.

Everything smelled delicious.

She went upstairs to put on a purple, long-sleeved maxi dress. She then slipped on a pair of matching purple ballet flats.

Maxwell arrived thirty minutes later with a huge bouquet of flowers.

"Something smells good," he told her when she stepped aside to let him enter the townhouse.

"Thank you," she said with a smile. "Everything should be ready soon."

"These are for you," Maxwell said, holding out the

flowers to her. "When I saw them, they reminded me of you."

She sniffed the colorful bouquet and said, "They're beautiful, Maxwell. Thank you."

Maxwell and Camille sat down at the dining room table to eat as soon as the food was ready.

He quickly blessed the food before they dived in.

Camille could feel Maxwell watching her. "Shouldn't you be concentrating on your food?" She was eager for him to try the drunken chicken she'd prepared. It was her mother's recipe and one that usually turned out well when she cooked it.

"I can't believe we're here like this," he confessed.

Maxwell's eyes traveled over her face, and then slid downward. "When I came to Alexandria, I never expected to meet or start caring about anyone. I came here to help Hopewell's legal counsel with the Matthews lawsuit—that was it."

She took a sip of her lemonade. Camille felt a wave of apprehension course through her veins. She wasn't really sure where Maxwell was going with his conversation.

He met her gaze straight on. "I guess what I'm trying to say is that I never expected to develop feelings for you. I care about you, Camille."

Camille wiped her mouth with the edge of her napkin. "Since we're being honest, I want you to know that I really care about you, too."

The air around them suddenly seemed electrified.

Maxwell wiped his mouth with his napkin. "I believe we both know where this relationship is going, so there's something we should really talk about."

"What is it?" Camille tried to read his expression for a clue of what he wanted to discuss.

"When this case is wrapped up, I'll be returning to New York."

"I'm aware of that," she stated without emotion.

"How do you feel about that?"

"To be honest, I'm trying not to think about it," Camille confessed. "I just want to enjoy the time that we do have together."

He nodded in agreement. "I am a native New Yorker, Camille. I love the city and I intend to stay there."

"I understand," she said. "Maxwell, I don't have any false illusions about us."

Taking her hand in his, he said, "I don't want this to end. What we have together is something special. I want it to run its course."

"Are you telling me that you want to have a long-distance relationship?" Camille asked, seeking clarity.

"I do. For now." Maxwell grinned. "Hopefully I can persuade you to move to New York."

Camille gasped in surprise.

He laughed. "I'm sorry. I didn't mean to shock you."

It took a moment for her to find her voice. "I guess I just didn't expect something like that to come out of your mouth, especially at this point in our relationship."

"I surprised myself," he confessed. "But I mean it, Camille. I'm not looking for something temporary. I didn't really realize it until now." Maxwell met her gaze straight on. "How do you feel about this? Are we on the same page?"

Camille surveyed Maxwell's face, and then smiled. "I would like to see where this goes."

After they finished eating, Camille pushed away from the table and stood up. "Make yourself comfortable while I clean up the kitchen."

"I'll help," Maxwell offered.

She looked at him in disbelief. "Really? *You?*"

Maxwell kissed her. "I know how to cook, clean a house and wash dishes. I have a lot to offer a woman."

She laughed. "You sure do."

They put the dishes into the dishwasher and put away the rest of the food. When the kitchen was clean, they settled down on the living room sofa.

Maxwell pulled her into his arms, holding her close.

Camille laid her head against his chest. Whenever she was in his arms, there was only one way she could define how she felt—it was like coming home. It felt perfect. It felt right.

His mouth covered hers and she let herself respond to his kiss.

Camille pulled away slowly. "I have never felt this way before."

"Neither have I. The thought of losing you doesn't sit well with me."

Happiness welled up in her at his words. Camille could feel her heartbeat racing just from the sound of Maxwell's voice.

He kissed her again and this time full-out desire ignited in her belly. She felt as if she were losing herself in Maxwell. It was as if the two of them were destined to become lovers tonight.

She pulled away reluctantly. "I guess we should put the brakes on," she whispered.

"Really?"

She nodded. "I don't think we should rush into a…" Camille struggled to find the right words.

"A physical relationship," he finished for her.

"Yes," Camille responded. Nervous, she chewed on her bottom lip.

He eyed her lovingly. "I have to tell you, Camille.

You are a very sexy woman. You can't blame a man for trying."

"I find you incredibly sexy as well," she pulled his face down and whispered in his ear.

Turning in his arms, Camille lifted her mouth to him, kissing him softly. Unnamable sensations ran through her as Maxwell's hands traveled down her body. She felt the heat from their closeness, and her body began to burn with his touch.

Maxwell gently grasped Camille's hand, his fingers fondling its smoothness. When she looked up at him, her gaze sent currents through him.

He lowered his head and kissed her on the forehead. "I think I'd better go." He pulled her to her feet and into his arms.

He held her close to him. "I don't want to leave you."

"Maxwell, I really don't want you to go," Camille responded as a shiver of wanting ran down her spine. "But we should call it a night."

She walked him to the door.

"Good night," Camille said, her voice barely above a whisper. "I'll see you in the morning."

She watched from her window as he drove away.

Why did I let him leave?

Camille knew the answer already. It was because she was a virgin. She planned to tell him but only when the time was right.

Maxwell could not deny it any longer. He was falling in love with Camille.

Earlier tonight, Maxwell had been transparent with her about his feelings and wanting to pursue a relationship with her. He had never—

The telephone rang, interrupting his thoughts.

"Dad, thanks for calling me back." Maxwell was thrilled to hear from his father. He had been trying to connect with him for the past couple of days.

"I've been in court," his dad explained.

Their conversation was brief, but after talking to his father, Maxwell decided to fly home to New York for the rest of the week. He had to complete work on some of his other projects.

Maxwell smiled to himself as an idea formed in his mind.

I'm going to invite Camille to go to New York with me. It would give her a chance to see the city from my point of view.

Early the next morning, he sent Camille an email inviting her to have lunch with him.

Afterward, he and Ray went downstairs to try and catch up with Dr. Dudley. They needed to discuss some of the details of the lawsuit with him.

On his way back to the elevator, Maxwell saw Isabelle and stopped to say hello.

She pasted on a huge smile and said, "Hey, Maxwell. How are you doing?"

"Doing good," he responded.

Isabelle grabbed him by the arm, surprising him. Her voice low, she said, "Camille's my girl. I don't want you breaking her heart. Okay?"

He grinned. "I hear you, Dr. Morales."

Maxwell spotted Thomas and rushed to join him at the other end of the hallway.

"I guess whatever you said to Dudley worked," Thomas said. "He's having a new fraternization policy drafted."

"I just spoke to him and he never mentioned anything," Maxwell stated. "That's great news."

"I think so," Thomas replied. "Hey, how are things going with Camille?"

Hearing her name prompted a smile on his face. "I'm planning on inviting her to New York. I need to take care of some casework, so I'm flying out tomorrow morning."

Thomas looked surprised. "I guess things are going really well with you two."

"She's very special," Maxwell said.

Two hours later, he and Camille entered the hospital cafeteria. It was beginning to snow, so they decided to stay on-site.

"I have to go home for the rest of the week," Maxwell announced after they sat down at one of the tables near the windows. "I need to take care of some time-sensitive cases."

"When do you think you'll be back?" Camille inquired. She took a sip of her hot herbal tea.

"Not until Sunday evening."

"I'm going to miss you," she told him.

Maxwell sliced off a piece of his chicken. "I was actually hoping that you would join me, sweetheart. I'd like for you to come to New York."

Camille's eyes registered her surprise at his invitation. She didn't exactly know how to respond.

"I would love to show you around Manhattan. It's beautiful there this time of the year."

She smiled. "I haven't been to New York since I was a teen. Maxwell, I have to be honest. Your invitation really caught me by surprise. I would love to join you, but I need to check my calendar. The charity ball is weeks away and then there's the Christmas party for the kids—there's a lot going on."

Stunned, Maxwell blinked. He hadn't really expected her to say anything but yes. He was used to women jumping at his every whim. Most would have been thrilled to receive his invitation. Camille hadn't said no, but she hadn't said yes, either.

He gave himself a mental shake. "I'm not trying to rush you into anything you're not ready to do. I have several guest rooms."

Camille reached over, placing her hand over his. "Maxwell, it's nothing like that. This is just so unexpected."

"I just don't want you to think that I'm trying to get you away just to ravish you."

She laughed. "I don't think you'd do that. You're my knight in shining armor, remember? You saved me from you-know-who." Camille didn't want to say Dr. Dudley's name in the event someone was listening to their conversation.

"I hope that you'll decide to come with me," Maxwell said. "I know that we'd have a good time in New York."

She smiled. "As soon as I get back to my office, I'll check my calendar and let you know."

Maxwell didn't know if she was just playing it cool or if she really needed to consult her calendar. The fact that she had not jumped at his invitation bothered him to no end.

Chapter 10

Alone in her office, Camille was delighted by Maxwell's invitation to join him in New York. The idea of seeing the city all dressed up for Christmas was tempting, but she also knew that Maxwell was ready to take their relationship to the next level.

It wasn't that Camille wasn't ready for a physical relationship with him. He ignited sparks of desire within her whenever they were together, roused emotions that she had never felt with any other man. The truth was that she had never really been in love before. What she was experiencing with Maxwell was foreign to her. He was getting to her in ways no other man ever had.

Camille hadn't told him that she was still a virgin; the time was never right to have such a discussion. She wasn't one of the experienced and sophisticated women Maxwell was used to dating. She didn't even have the right clothes.

She loved the thought of being alone with Maxwell for a weekend, but she just didn't want to take the chance of making a fool out of herself in front of him.

He is a good man, Camille silently acknowledged. *He's been brutally honest with me, one of the reasons I've fallen so hard for him.*

Deep down, she really wanted to go to New York.

Camille picked up the phone to call Maxwell. She wanted to tell him that she would meet him in New York on Friday.

However, fear set in, forcing her to abandon the call. *What am I thinking? I can't do this.*

She got little work done as she debated whether or not to spend the weekend with Maxwell.

He was still heavy on her mind an hour later, but Camille was no closer to a decision. She clasped her hands to her head and groaned. "I can't believe this. It shouldn't be so hard."

Reaching for the telephone, she muttered, "This is so crazy. I should go to New York with him."

Camille hung up the phone before Maxwell could answer. "No, I can't...."

She inhaled deeply and exhaled slowly.

Picking up the receiver, Camille dialed quickly before she changed her mind. "Maxwell, do you have a minute to talk?"

"Sure," he responded. "What's up?"

"I want to talk to you about the trip to New York."

She hung up the phone after Maxwell volunteered to come to her office for their discussion.

Her assistant had already left for lunch, so they would be free of interruption.

Camille was seated on the sofa in her office when Maxwell arrived. "Thanks for coming down," she said.

He sat down beside her. "What's up, sweetheart?"

Her hands folded in her lap, Camille cleared her throat nervously. "Maxwell, I've been thinking about your invitation. I considered meeting you there on Friday, but…" Her voice died.

"But what?"

"I think it's best if I decline this time around," she said. "I still have a lot to do on the charity ball and some other projects." She gave him a tiny smile. "I really hope you'll ask me again some other time."

She had not been prepared for how disappointed Maxwell looked. "There will be other times, won't there?" Camille asked.

"Of course," Maxwell responded after a brief pause. "Can you tell me something, Camille? What's the real reason you're turning me down?"

"I assure you it's all work-related." She couldn't tell him that the real reason she declined had to do with her insecurities.

Maxwell wore a look of disbelief, but he didn't argue.

Camille kissed him. "I'm going to miss you."

"It doesn't have to be this way," he said softly. "You could come with me."

"Maxwell, I have so much on my plate right now. I really can't leave as much as I want to spend time with you."

"Your assistant can't take over for you?" he asked. "It's just a few days."

Camille shook her head. She felt terrible for lying to him like this, but it couldn't be helped. She was just as disappointed, but felt she was doing the right thing.

"Hey, why don't I make dinner for you tonight?" Camille suggested. "We could stay in and watch a movie."

"Sounds nice," he told her.

"Maxwell…"

"I'm sorry," he said. "I'm just disappointed. I was really looking forward to showing you New York at Christmastime. I was looking forward to having you all to myself. Away from any distractions."

Camille almost gave in to his silent pleading. When he boarded his jet tomorrow, she would not see him for five days. To her heart, it sounded like an eternity.

Maxwell did not believe for one minute that it was Camille's job that was keeping her from joining him in New York. He didn't know the real reason for her turning him down. Maybe she wasn't ready to take their relationship to the next level. Maybe Camille wasn't as attracted to him as she had led him to believe. For the first time in his life, he doubted his appeal.

He was frustrated. Maxwell was used to women catering to him. He was the one who never lacked the attention of females. They were honored to be seen on his arm.

What was wrong with Camille? Why didn't she see him the same way other women did?

Maxwell surprised himself with the way he was reacting to Camille's denial. Maybe it was actually for the best that she had turned him down. His feelings were escalating too quickly.

I need to take it slower, he decided. He vowed to take the next five days to rethink his relationship with Camille. The last thing he wanted to do was rush into another relationship like he did with Kendra. That mistake had taken several years to undo.

Maxwell picked up the telephone and called Camille.

"Hey, I've decided to fly out this evening, so I guess I'll see you in five days."

"Do you really have to leave tonight?" she asked.

"If I go ahead and leave from the hospital, I can get an early start tomorrow morning. I'll call you when I get home."

"Maxwell, I'm going to miss you," Camille told him. "It's not going to be the same without you here."

He loved the sound of her voice. Surprisingly he was already missing her. There was some part of him that wanted to hang up and rush to her office, to wrap his arms around her and kiss her.

His body ached for Camille. He wanted her badly, but it was pretty obvious that she did not feel the same way.

Maxwell reminded himself that Camille was different from most women he dated in so many ways. She didn't hang on his every word or cater to him as he was used to women doing. Camille hadn't tried to seduce him or use her female wiles to manipulate him.

It was refreshing.

Camille was a breath of fresh air. He loved that he could just be himself around her. She had no expectations of expensive gifts, exotic vacations or anything like that. She wasn't demanding of his time.

Maxwell couldn't deny it. Camille was perfect for him and he couldn't see his life without her in it.

I love her.

He definitely needed to take some time to sort out his feelings. While he cared deeply for her, he wasn't sure he was ready for a serious relationship with anyone.

He thought about Kendra and shook his head. He had to be sure this time around. Life with his ex-girlfriend had been hell. He was too old to deal with more drama.

The telephone rang, drawing him out of his turbulent thoughts.

It was his father's secretary.

Maxwell confirmed his travel plans with her, and then hung up the phone. He felt instant regret over changing his flight plans. *There's no way I can get on the jet without seeing Camille.*

He pushed away from his desk. He was about to head to Camille's office when she suddenly appeared in his doorway, surprising him.

"I couldn't let you leave without seeing you," she said. "I felt like…I had to see you."

"I was on my way to your office," he responded. "I needed to see you, too."

They laughed.

Maxwell wished he could've gotten through to Camille and had been able to convince her to come with him. His body yearned to be close to hers.

"So when do you plan to leave for the airport?" Camille inquired.

"I'm leaving shortly," he said.

"I'm glad I came by," she told him. "I didn't know you were leaving so soon."

"I'm trying not to make it harder on myself," Maxwell confessed. It was true.

The thought of leaving Camille behind saddened him.

He wondered if she was afraid to trust him. "Camille, I want you to know that I would never do anything to hurt you."

She smiled. "I know that, Maxwell."

Camille reached over and took him by the hand. "I have a lot of work that needs to be completed."

"Are you sure that's all it is?"

Smiling, she answered, "Yes. As far as I'm concerned, what we have together is perfect. I'm very happy with you, Maxwell."

He grinned. "Same here."

He wanted to believe that they were on the same page, but doubt continued to nag at him.

"Camille, what is wrong with you, girl?" Jerome questioned when he spied her on the first floor the next morning. "You look like you've lost your best friend."

"You're my best friend," she responded with a sigh. "But I may have lost Maxwell."

They walked over to an empty waiting area to talk without fear of being overheard.

"Did you two have a fight?" Jerome inquired.

Camille shook her head no. "He has to take care of some business in New York and he invited me to go with him."

"So when are you two leaving?"

"That's just it," Camille stated. "He's already gone. Jerome, I turned him down."

Jerome shook his head in disbelief.

"What?" Camille asked.

"You got the one man that half the women in this hospital are drooling over, wanting to spend some time with you and what do you do? You tell him no."

She gave a slight shrug. "It's not like I have any real experience, Jerome. I am not about to go all the way to New York just to end up disappointing the man."

Frowning, Jerome questioned, "Girl, what are you talking about?"

Camille met his gaze. "Jerome, I'm a… I've never…"

Jerome's mouth dropped open in surprise. *"You're a virgin?"*

She folded her arms across her chest. "You don't

have to make it sound like a bad thing. I'm not going to apologize for not jumping into bed with some man who will most likely forget my name twenty-four hours later."

"Honey, I didn't mean it like that. I'm just shocked, that's all." He scratched his head. "I don't think I've ever known a virgin."

Camille rolled her eyes at him. "See, this is why I didn't go to New York. Most men would probably have your reaction."

Jerome shook his head. "I don't believe you didn't go just because you're a virgin, Camille. C'mon, what's the real reason?"

She walked over to an empty chair near the window and sat down. "Jerome, I'm not sophisticated like the women Maxwell is used to dating. Hey, I sleep in a pair of old sweats and a T-shirt." Camille sat with her shoulders slumped.

"Okay, this is what we're going to do, Camille. We're leaving work early today," Jerome announced. "I'm taking you shopping."

"It's too late," she said. "Maxwell left yesterday."

"How long will he be gone?"

"Five long days," Camille responded. "I know it sounds crazy, but I really miss him."

"Well we're going shopping and then I'm taking you to the airport on Friday. You *are* going to New York."

She shook her head. "I can't do that, Jerome. I already told him that I wasn't coming."

"You're going to surprise him."

Camille had mixed feelings about traveling to New York without alerting Maxwell of her visit.

"Are you sure about this?" she asked Jerome. "You

really think I should go there without saying a word to Maxwell?"

"That's the whole purpose of it being a surprise."

Camille gave him a sharp jab in the arm. "Stop being such a smart mouth."

He laughed. "Smart mouth? See, that's why people think you are such a goody-goody. Have you ever just broken down and given someone a good cussing out?"

"No. Not really."

"Some people need to be cussed out," Jerome pointed out. "Like Miss Thang. She won't act right until I cuss her out."

Camille chuckled. "I'm going back to my office. I'll see you around three-fifteen. We can head out then."

"See ya," Jerome said. He walked in the direction of the outpatient surgery department. He was filling in for a nurse who was out sick and was getting off when his relief arrived at 3:00 p.m.

Right on time they left work and headed to the mall.

Camille drove her car and Jerome followed behind in his.

At the first department store Camille held up a striped banded-style dress in black. "What do you think about this one, Jerome?"

He eyed the skimpy outfit in her hand and said, "I like it, but not in black. You wear black all of the time. Get the red one. Be daring."

Camille laughed. "You're trying to turn me into the type of women you date."

"Hey, that's why I'm here. You want to know what men like seeing on their women. Well, the red one is it. I'm telling you that Maxwell will love that dress on you."

Camille wrinkled up her face. "You really think so?"

He nodded. "Trust me, this was made for you."

She still wasn't convinced. "Maybe I should get it in a bigger size, though. I think this one might be a little too tight for me."

Jerome stilled her hand. "This dress was made to hug your curves. Camille, this is the type of outfit your man wants to see on you."

"I don't know about this, Jerome." Camille chewed on her bottom lip. She wanted to look sexy for Maxwell, but she didn't want to appear too easy or look like a tramp.

"I'm going to pass on that one," she finally decided. "It's just not me."

After walking around and finding nothing to Camille's taste, they moved on to another store that was one of her favorite places to shop.

Camille removed a dress from a nearby rack. "Now this looks more like me."

Jerome had to agree.

It was a beautiful raspberry color, and while understated, it was also sexy. Camille found her size and tried it on.

When she strolled out of the dressing room, Jerome nodded in approval. "Perfect."

They continued shopping for other outfits. Camille slowed her pace, pausing to check the price of a shirt on one of the racks. "Jerome, I have to tell you something."

"What is it?" he said, eyeing the girl at the makeup counter.

"I'm in love with Maxwell."

He broke into a smile. "I can tell. You have the look of a woman in love. That said, we need to head over here."

Camille followed Jerome into the lingerie department. She stopped at a rack of lacy, racy items. "This is gorgeous."

Jerome nodded. "I need to get one of these for my honey."

"Wow, it costs a pretty penny, too," Camille murmured.

"You put that on and you're going to blow Maxwell's mind. He will forget all about your being a virgin."

She smiled.

It *was* nice, but it left nothing to the imagination.

Jerome removed it off the rack and stuck it in Camille's hand. "Maxwell is going to love it!"

She picked up another item and ran her fingers across the delicate braiding and velvet trimming. "I'm going to get this one, too," she told Jerome.

When she and Jerome finished, Camille marched up to the cashier and paid for her purchases. In all, she had spent her paycheck for the month, but didn't feel any regret.

Nor did she when Jerome surprised her the next afternoon by treating her to a facial and makeover.

"I feel like a whole new person," she told him afterward.

"You look good, girl," Jerome complimented. "Don't get me wrong, you always look good, but you have this glow about you now."

"I can't believe that I'm doing this."

"You are," Jerome confirmed. "While I was waiting on you, I booked your flight to New York and arranged to have a car waiting for you when you land. Camille, you're all set."

She met his gaze. "This is really happening, huh?"

He nodded.

Camille was ecstatic. In less than ten hours, she would be on a plane heading to New York.

Camille eyed her reflection in the mirror.

She had to admit she liked the new mineral makeup and the way it felt on her skin. She ran her hand down the side of the formfitting dress, loving the feel of the soft fabric. It wasn't tight; instead the garment hugged her curves lovingly.

Camille checked her watch. It was time to head to the airport.

She slipped on her calf-length leather coat, which matched the boots she was wearing, and grabbed her purse and overnight bag.

I'm on my way to you, Maxwell.

Camille prayed that he would be happy to see her. They had talked last night for almost two hours. She had been tempted to tell him about her trip, but changed her mind.

She arrived at the airport and within the hour was boarding the plane. She was pretty sure traveling by private jet was much more comfortable than a commercial flight, but Camille would've flown by carrier pigeon if she had to. She couldn't wait to see Maxwell.

On the plane, she pulled a book out of her tote and began reading. She was relieved that there had been no delays and that they would be taking off soon.

She fell asleep midway, but woke just as the plane was preparing to land. A wave of apprehension swept through her, but she shook it off. She had come too far to chicken out now.

Chapter 11

Maxwell was frustrated beyond measure.

He had called Camille three times in the last couple of hours. He thought maybe she was working late, but when he called the office, he found out that she had not come in at all.

She had lied to him.

Maxwell didn't want to believe it, but could come up with no other reason. He had called her home and her cell phone. Each time, there was no answer—just an automated voice instructing him to leave a message.

"What is going on with her?" he whispered in the empty room.

When they talked last night, Maxwell did not detect that anything was wrong between them. Another thought he hadn't considered until now struck him.

Maybe she was seeing another man.

The thought of Camille with another man disturbed Maxwell deeply.

She wouldn't do that to me, he kept telling himself. *Would she?*

Maxwell's mood shifted and veered toward anger when he called her again. She was still not picking up. He and Camille needed to have a serious conversation as soon as he returned to Virginia, he decided.

It was not a conversation he wanted to have over the phone. Maxwell wanted to see her face. He would know if she was telling the truth. After all, he had been trained to discern if he was being lied to. He had trusted Camille up until this point.

She had never given him any reason not to do so.

A thread of guilt slid down his back.

There could be a number of reasons why Camille wasn't answering her phone that didn't have to do with another man. She was nothing like Kendra and he was wrong for assuming that she would go running out on him while he was out of town.

Maxwell wasn't sure he could handle the pressures of a long-distance relationship. This was the first time Camille had been out of contact, and he was already accusing her of cheating on him.

What was love without trust?

"This is it," the driver said to Camille. They were parked in front of an impressive building made of contoured steel that seemed to dominate the skyline.

"Thank you," she murmured. Camille eyed the building with a mixture of awe and trepidation.

The chauffer got out and walked around the car to open the door for her. Camille paid him and thanked him a second time.

As she walked toward Maxwell's condo, Camille whispered, "Why did I let Jerome talk me into coming here?"

Gathering her courage, she walked up to the building, pausing for a moment to inhale the night air.

I might as well get this over with, she thought to herself.

As she neared the door, Camille took a step forward, and then hesitated. She glanced around, her heart racing. "I don't think I can do this."

For a split second, she felt like running off, but reality took over. Camille didn't know much about Manhattan, so she had no choice but to dispel all discomfort. She had come all the way here to see Maxwell, and she was going through with it.

What if he was not home?

Fear welled up in her and tears sprang in her eyes. She had no place to go. *What was I thinking by coming to New York without telling Maxwell?*

"Miss, can I help you?" a man in uniform asked.

Camille swallowed her apprehension. "I'm here to see Maxwell Wade," she managed to get out.

He held the door open for her to enter. "Is Mr. Wade expecting you?"

"Yes," she blurted out without thinking.

He walked over to the desk and made a phone call. Camille assumed he was verifying the information with Maxwell.

It seemed like an eternity before he instructed her to go up to Maxwell's penthouse.

When the elevator doors opened, Maxwell was standing there, bare-chested and gorgeous.

Without preamble, he pulled her into his arms. "I can't believe you're here."

Camille looked up at him. "So you're not mad at me for not telling you that I was coming?"

Maxwell shook his head. "I called you last night and this morning. I was beginning to worry when I never heard back from you."

"I got your messages and your texts," she told him. "I just really wanted to surprise you."

He covered her mouth with his, kissing her passionately.

"Maybe we should go inside your place," she whispered again his chest. The initial fear she had experienced evaporated once she was in his arms.

Inside the penthouse, Camille removed her coat.

Maxwell surveyed her from head to toe. "I see that you had more than one surprise in store for me. Are there any more?"

"Maybe," she replied cryptically.

Maxwell was thrilled to see her, so Camille was able to relax.

When he caught her eyeing his bare chest, Maxwell explained, "I just got out of the shower and was about to get dressed. I had planned to go to the office, but I think I'll work from home today," Maxwell told her. "Hey, are you hungry?"

"Yes," she responded.

"I'll make us some breakfast. Do you have a desire for anything special?"

"No. Just surprise me." Camille didn't care what they ate. She was reveling in the joy of being with the man she loved. The look on his face when he saw her warmed her all over.

While Maxwell was in the bathroom, Camille studied her reflection once more. She was pleased to see how much he loved her dress. She'd have to find a couple more similar in style.

Maxwell came out of the bathroom completely dressed.

"I decided to order something instead of cooking," he announced. "It should be here in about fifteen minutes." He paused a moment before asking, "Unless you wanted to go out to eat?"

Camille shook her head.

He just kept staring at her. It was as if Maxwell could not believe that she was actually there.

She walked over to Maxwell and wrapped her arms around him. "I'm really here."

He held her close to him. "I'm so glad to see you. I missed you, baby."

"I missed you, too. Five days doesn't seem like a long time until you're separated from someone you truly care about."

He agreed with her.

The food arrived sooner than expected, and Maxwell blessed it and they sat down to eat. He had ordered Belgian waffles, scrambled eggs, fresh fruit and turkey sausage for them.

"You don't have to stay home if you need to be at your office," Camille said. "I don't mind staying here and catching up on some reading."

"My assistant can bring the files over," Maxwell said with a shrug. "I want to spend as much time as I can with you."

They made small talk as they finished their breakfast.

Camille offered to clean up, but he refused her assistance. "You're here to be spoiled and pampered this weekend," Maxwell stated. "I am going to cater to you."

She smiled in gratitude.

His assistant arrived an hour later with files for Maxwell. He introduced Camille to the woman who had worked for him for the past ten years. She reminded him about an upcoming dinner on Saturday night, honoring his father.

Maxwell had clearly forgotten all about it.

After his assistant left, he turned to Camille and asked, "I don't suppose you brought a gown or a cocktail dress with you?"

"I didn't, but I can buy one," she responded.

Maxwell picked up the phone. "I'm going to order a car for you. There's a shop that my mother loves not too far from here. Pick out whatever you want and have the manager put it on my account."

"You don't have to do that," Camille interjected. "I can pay for it."

"Honey, I want to do this for you," Maxwell insisted.

After a short pause, she gave in. "Thank you."

"Thank me *after* you find something."

"Your home is really beautiful," Camille murmured as she looked around. She had never been in a place so well appointed with custom furniture and so beautifully decorated.

"Thanks. I can't take credit for it, though. My mother sent over her decorator—it was her housewarming gift to me."

Maxwell gave her a quick tour of the penthouse, which featured picturesque views from all of the rooms. The private garden deck was perfect for entertaining. His home also boasted a library, family room, eat-in kitchen, four spacious bedrooms and a formal dining room.

"I also have two rooms for staff," Maxwell said.

Camille turned around to face him. "Do you have live-in staff?"

He shook his head. "I value my privacy. I do have a housekeeper who comes in to clean once a week, though."

After the tour, Camille went into one of the bathrooms to freshen up while Maxwell made a couple of phone calls.

When the car arrived that would take her to the boutique, he helped her with her coat and escorted her downstairs.

"I won't be gone long," Camille promised before getting into the car.

"Take your time, sweetheart," Maxwell said. "I'll be here waiting for you."

He kissed her once more, and then sent Camille on her way.

Maxwell felt like a heel.

He had basically accused Camille of having an affair, but apparently she was on her way to surprise him. She complimented him on his penthouse, but did not seem impressed by its grandeur. Camille was comfortable in her own skin and did not worship material possessions like most of the women he had dated in the past.

I don't deserve a woman like Camille.

She hadn't told him how she felt about him, but Maxwell was pretty sure that her feelings mirrored his. Seeing her away from Hopewell General—away from the lawsuit, the sexual harassment and the planning of the charity ball—Camille seemed like a different person.

Although he yearned to make love to her, Maxwell was not going to assume that they would connect on an intimate level during this visit. He decided to place her in the guest room across from his room. He was open to whatever might happen between them.

He was still thinking about her when Camille returned to the penthouse two hours later.

She showed him the dress that she purchased but refused to model it. "You will just have to wait until tomorrow night," she stated.

Maxwell gave her a mock look of disappointment, prompting a short laugh out of Camille. "It's not going to work."

"I'm almost at a point where I can stop working," he announced. "We'll go out for lunch in about an hour."

"That's fine."

He took the dress out of her hands. "I'll hang this up for you."

Camille wrapped her arms around Maxwell when he returned a few minutes later. She laid her head on his chest and he inhaled the scent that he'd come to know as Camille's. They stood there without saying a word. He wasn't ready to verbalize his feelings yet.

An hour later, Maxwell took Camille to a Japanese restaurant, where she surveyed the dimly lit surroundings and the romantic ambiance. Because she was unfamiliar with the food, he ordered for them both.

"Were you able to get a lot done?" she asked Maxwell while they sipped their beverages.

"I actually got quite a bit done," Maxwell responded.

"I'd like to see you in action in court one day." Camille took a sip of her ice water. "I know that you're a fantastic attorney."

"I've grown to love my job," he said.

"I thought about studying law at one point," Camille said. "Then I considered going to school to be a pediatrician. But then I was interested in marketing so that's what I studied at Virginia Union."

Maxwell met her gaze. "I think you would've made a great lawyer."

Camille shrugged. "Maybe. I love my job at the hospital, so I'm in the right field, at least at this point in my life."

When the waiter brought their lunches, Maxwell said the blessing and Camille sampled sushi for the first time in her life.

"Well, how do you like it?" Maxwell asked.

"It's delicious," she responded. She wiped her mouth with the edge of her napkin. "I didn't think I was going to like raw fish." She smiled and Maxwell couldn't keep his observation to himself.

"You look even more beautiful when you smile," he told her, taking her hand in his. "I love the way your green eyes sparkle."

Then he couldn't help it. He gave her a look that, judging from her expression, was filled with all the emotion—all the lust—he felt.

Camille was fighting her own battle, trying to keep her passion under control. She was curious about how it would be when the time came for them to make love.

When the time was right, she had to tell him her secret. She prayed her lack of experience would not become a turnoff for him.

She hadn't been in New York one full day yet, but so far everything was perfect.

Even the afternoon back at the penthouse went well. She took a nap for an hour, and then curled up in the library with her book while Maxwell finished up his work.

He met her in there at about four-thirty.

Camille grinned at him. "Are you finished?"

Yes," Maxwell responded. "Now I can give you all of my attention."

He pulled Camille to her feet. "So, pretty lady, what do you want to do now?"

"I don't have anything in mind," she told him. "Being here with you like this is enough for me."

Maxwell hugged her. "I was thinking that we could do some shopping tomorrow. I know that you haven't finished your Christmas shopping yet. I still have a few items to get."

"Great," she murmured.

"We can go out to dinner tonight or we can stay in," Maxwell stated. "It's your choice, sweetheart."

"Let's stay inside tonight."

"Are you sure?" he inquired. "I feel as if I'm being very selfish."

Camille met his gaze straight on. "I love it, Maxwell. I'm glad you want to keep me all to yourself."

Maxwell took her by the hand and led her into the living room. They sat down to finish their conversation.

"I really didn't think I'd see you this weekend," he told her. "I thought maybe I was going too fast for you. I thought I'd scared you away."

"No, you haven't scared me off, Maxwell. I wasn't sure I should come to New York because I didn't want you to think that I was easy or loose. But I'm really glad that I came," Camille confessed. "I have to admit that I was nervous about coming."

He seemed surprised. "Really?"

She gave a slight nod.

"Why were you so nervous?" Maxwell questioned.

Camille twisted her hands in her lap. "You're used to

dating women who are gorgeous and very sophisticated. I'm more of a tomboy."

Maxwell took her hand in his. "Sweetheart, I like you just the way that you are. You are a refreshing change from the women I usually date."

Their gaze met and held.

"I wouldn't trade you for any of those women," Maxwell stated.

His words brought a smile to her lips.

She was still smiling an hour later when they made dinner together, choosing a simple meal to prepare. Maxwell kept her laughing.

She hadn't laughed so hard and for so long in a while. Camille enjoyed seeing this comedic side of Maxwell. He continued to surprise her.

After dinner, they settled down and watched a movie together. Camille laid her head against Maxwell's chest. She wasn't sure how much of the movie she actually saw. She spent most of the time thinking about him and how much she was enjoying being in his arms.

She couldn't have asked for a better evening.

Unfortunately, around eleven-thirty it was time to retire for the evening.

Maxwell escorted her to the guest room across from his. "I didn't want you to feel that you have to rush into a physical relationship with me. I'm willing to wait until you feel that you're ready."

Camille smiled at him. "You never cease to surprise me."

"Good night, sweetheart." He touched his lips to hers.

"Good night," she murmured in response.

Camille opened her door and stepped into the bedroom. At the far end of the room, a floor-to-ceiling window gifted her with a looking glass to the beauty of Manhattan at night.

She crossed the varnished hardwood floor in bare feet toward the rich mahogany bed that framed a silver-gray comforter and several jewel-toned pillows.

Camille sat down on the bed and leaned back against the stack of pillows adorning the king-size headboard. She was deeply touched that Maxwell had not just assumed they would be sleeping together.

She slipped into the black lacy gown Jerome had talked her into buying. Camille felt a wave of disappointment that Maxwell would not get a chance to see it on her.

She climbed into bed, but felt too restless to sleep. Twenty minutes later she got up and strode over to the window, letting her gaze drift over the moonlit sky.

In the quiet, the soft knock on her door startled her.

"Maxwell?" she called out.

He stuck his head inside. "It's me. I heard you moving about, so I thought I'd check on you."

She awarded him a tiny smile. "I couldn't sleep."

Walking inside the room, Maxwell's eyes traveled from her face, to her neck, and continued downward. "You look stunning," he whispered.

He was bare-chested and the light from the moon cast a soft glow over his firm muscles. Camille moved toward him as if drawn by an invisible thread.

Maxwell traced his fingertip across her lip causing her skin to tingle when he touched her. He paused to kiss her, sending currents of desire through her.

"I've tried to fight my feelings, sweetheart, but it's a losing battle. I want to make love to you," he whispered in her ear.

"There's something you should know," she began.

He cut her off by saying, "Camille, I don't know when it happened, but I've fallen in love with you. I'm not saying this because I want to get you in bed. If you don't want to make love, we don't have to do anything. That's why I put you here in the guest room. I don't want you to feel any pressure."

His declaration of love brought tears of happiness to her eyes. "Maxwell, I love you, too."

He gently wiped away her tears. "You're so good for me."

Pulling her into his arms, he said, "You look so incredibly sexy."

"So do you," Camille whispered. "Maxwell, there's something I have to tell you. I've… I am a…"

"What is it, sweetheart?"

"When we make love, it will be my first time…ever. *You* will be my first, Maxwell."

"You're a virgin?" he asked, his tone gentle.

She nodded.

"Honey, we don't have to rush into this," Maxwell assured her. "I love you and we have all the time in the world."

"Do you really mean that?"

He nodded. "When we make love, I want to it to be perfect for you." His lips found hers, his touch igniting a fire in her belly.

"Make love to me," she whispered between kisses.

Maxwell groaned softly. "You don't know how badly I've wanted to hear those words come out of your mouth," he confessed. "I've wanted you from the moment I saw you."

Maxwell bent his head and captured her lips in a demanding kiss. Locking her hands behind his neck, Camille returned his kiss, matching his fire.

Her passion soaring, she allowed Maxwell to undress her.

His breath seemed to catch at the sight of her nudeness.

"You are so beautiful," he told her in a husky voice.

Maxwell removed his pajama bottoms and joined her in the bed. His mouth covered hers again hungrily.

Moaning, Camille drew herself closer to him as his hands explored her inexperienced body.

Maxwell slipped on a condom to protect them both, accepting the precious gift she offered. As the clock struck midnight, he took Camille as his own. Her body melted against his. The golden wave of pleasure and love flowed between them and the degree to which she responded stunned Camille.

She never knew making love to a man could feel this good.

Chapter 12

Maxwell and Camille spent most of Saturday Christmas shopping and sightseeing until it was time for them to get ready for the evening fundraiser, where his father would be giving the keynote address.

He openly admired the black cocktail dress Camille was wearing and beamed his approval. They sat with his mother while his father stood up on the dais, looking as if he owned the world. He delivered an incredible speech and received a standing ovation in return.

Constance Wade leaned over and whispered to Camille, "My husband spent most of the day working on that speech. He's changed it at least four times."

"He's an eloquent speaker," Camille responded.

"Maxwell is a gifted speaker as well," his mother said.

"I haven't heard him yet, but I have no doubt." Camille took a sip of her hot tea. She didn't care much for coffee, so she'd asked the waiter to bring her some hot water and a tea bag.

When the event was over, Maxwell and Camille followed his parents to their brownstone. His mother wanted to spend more time getting to know Camille. It pleased Maxwell that they were enjoying one another. His father had also made it known that he thought Camille was a better match for him than Kendra ever was.

They returned to Maxwell's penthouse shortly after eleven and spent the rest of the evening enjoying each other.

Maxwell watched her sleep, his heart overflowing with love. He resisted the urge to pinch himself. Camille almost seemed too good to be true.

I am a lucky man.

His cell phone began to vibrate on his nightstand.

Maxwell saw Kendra's name on the caller ID. He didn't answer.

He was not going to let her ruin his weekend. Hopefully, she had no idea about his being home. Maxwell did not want Kendra showing up and causing a scene. He definitely did not want to end up on her reality TV show.

Camille stirred but did not wake up.

He decided to turn the phone off, and then crawled back beneath the covers. Maxwell closed his eyes, but didn't fall asleep right away.

Kendra's phone call had disrupted what had been a blissful evening.

On Sunday morning, Maxwell woke up early and went downstairs to prepare something for Camille. He planned to surprise Camille with a delicious breakfast in bed.

"Did you cook all this?" she asked, when he brought the tray up an hour later.

Maxwell nodded. "I did. I told you that I knew how to cook. This is my chance to really impress you."

She lifted the sterling silver cover and surveyed the food. "You made the Belgian waffles this time? They didn't come from the restaurant?"

"Honey, I'm telling you the truth," Maxwell insisted as he sat down beside her on the bed. "I made them this morning. Wait until you see the kitchen."

They finished up breakfast, and then showered together.

He had really enjoyed having Camille with him in New York. Their relationship had gone to another level and their bond was solid. She had come to own his heart.

"I'm so glad I came to New York," Camille was saying. "I had a wonderful time being here with you."

Maxwell turned around to face her. "I'm really happy that you decided to come, Camille. I think we needed this time away from Virginia and the hospital."

She agreed.

That night while lying in bed with Camille asleep in his arms, Maxwell tried to recall if he'd ever been as happy as he was now. He had been happy with Kendra for the first year or so of their relationship, but after that, it had become fleeting.

She turned in his arms.

His body responded to the silky feel of her skin against his.

Maxwell planted tiny kisses along her cheek and her neck to wake her up.

Camille moaned softly.

He continued his slow seduction until she opened her eyes.

They soon connected in a sensual dance that lovers do, the union igniting fireworks that they both experienced.

Afterward, Maxwell continued to hold her close as they slept, satiated from the fulfillment of desire.

Eight hours later, they were up and ready to board Maxwell's private jet to Virginia.

"I wish we had one more day to stay in New York," Camille told him after they'd gotten settled on the jet.

"How about we come back next weekend?" he suggested. "We can spend our weekends in New York, if that's what you want to do."

"Really?" she asked with a smile.

"Provided the weather works in our favor."

"The idea sounds really wonderful, but with the charity ball so close, I will need to stay in Virginia. Once the fundraiser is over, my weekends will be free."

Maxwell smiled. "I love you, baby."

She reached over and took his hand in hers. "I love you, too."

Camille was absolutely giddy with happiness.

Maxwell loved her just as much as she loved him. It was truly a dream come true. She owed Jerome a special gift because the decision to go to New York had been the right choice. She never would've made it if it hadn't been for the persistence of her best friend.

Smiling, she stared out of the window while Maxwell reviewed some information from his briefcase.

"What are you thinking about, sweetheart?" he asked, intruding on her thoughts.

"I'm really happy," she responded.

He kissed her cheek. "So am I."

"How much more time before we land?" she inquired as she pulled her book out of her tote.

"Twenty minutes." He reached over and took her hand.

As soon as the jet landed, he and Camille were escorted to a waiting car. They headed straight to the hospital.

The moment they strolled into the hospital, Maxwell and Camille seemed to draw everyone's attention to them.

Camille's voice drifted into a hushed whisper. "I never realized just how nosy my coworkers are."

He chuckled.

When the elevator arrived and doors opened, Maxwell and Camille stepped inside.

"You know we really could've given them something to talk about," Maxwell suggested as he planted a sensual kiss on her lips. "Something that would've had them talking for many more years to come. You could've come in with your hair messed up and my tie could've been askew.…"

Camille gave a short laugh. "You're so bad."

They rode to the second floor and got off.

"I'll see you around noon for lunch," Maxwell told her.

"Okay," she responded with a smile.

Camille spent most of her morning in her office on a conference call with a prospective donor.

Fifteen minutes before she was scheduled to meet Maxwell for lunch, Jerome stopped by her office.

He dropped down on the sofa, saying, "So how was your weekend, Camille? Or is it Ms. Hunter now?"

She laughed. "I'm still me, Jerome. As for my

weekend in New York, it was wonderful. To be honest, I didn't want to come back home so soon."

"Loving New York or loving that man?" Jerome asked.

Camille grinned. "Both."

"Look at you," he said with a chuckle. "My baby is a grown woman now."

She threw a pencil at him. "Hush."

"Don't be ashamed," he teased. "Hey, you're out there doing grown-folk things. Be grown, girl."

"Go back to work, Jerome, before you get in trouble with Nurse Tsang."

He shrugged. "What is she going to do to me? I've been here longer than she has."

"She's still your supervisor," Camille pointed out.

"That's only because she's got the chief in her bed," Jerome retorted.

Camille shook her head. "You and that hospital grapevine. You have to know that half of what you hear probably isn't true."

Jerome rose to his feet. "Well, you know it's buzzing about you and Maxwell."

"I'm too happy to care what anybody has to say about us," Camille stated with a shrug. "Let them talk."

He smiled. "That's my girl. Go Cami… Go Cami…"

She burst into laughter. "You are so crazy. Hey, how are things between you and Julie?"

"Good," he responded. "We're still hanging out. I have to tell you, I really like this girl. She doesn't demand a lot of my time and she's secure."

"Just what you've been looking for," Camille said.

He nodded with a grin. "You know I need my space."

Camille leaned back in her chair. "I like Julie. She's perfect for you from what I can see."

He agreed.

Jerome checked his watch. "I guess I need to get moving. Hey, I'm happy for you, girl."

"Thanks," she responded. "I'm happy for us both."

"Now that you have a man, don't think you can just forget about your best friend."

Camille met his gaze. "Jerome, you know that I would never do that. Besides, you would never let me get away with something like that."

He chuckled. "You're right about that."

They could hear Dr. Dudley's voice in the hallway.

Jerome made a face. "Watch this. In about five minutes, you will see Miss Thang come down the hall."

Camille sent him a sharp look. Before she could voice her thoughts, Nurse Tsang walked by, her steps determined.

"What did I tell you?" Jerome asked.

Her mouth dropped open in shock.

Jerome rose to his feet and strode to the door. "I'll see you later."

"Bye," Camille responded. She had heard from Maxwell that Dr. Dudley and Nurse Tsang were having an affair, but Camille hadn't wanted to believe it.

"Oh well," she whispered. "It's really none of my business."

She turned on her computer monitor and decided to focus on her work.

Shortly after twelve noon, Camille checked her watch, and then touched up her sheer lip gloss. She was about to have lunch with the man she loved.

When they returned, Jaclyn ran over to them, saying, "Camille, you are never going to believe what happened. We got our Christmas miracle."

Momentarily confused, Camille glanced up at Maxwell. She didn't have any idea what Jaclyn was talking about.

"My patient, Robert Waterford—" Jaclyn began.

"Oh, the man who was in a coma," Camille interjected. "Did he come out of it?"

Jaclyn nodded. "His wife decided to give in to the son and daughter. We turned off the ventilator and Mr. Waterford began to breathe on his own. He opened his eyes about fifteen minutes ago."

"That's wonderful," Camille said. "The controversy actually resolved itself." She was thrilled for the hospital and for the patient.

"That's good news," Maxwell chimed in.

Camille and Jaclyn embraced.

"That's one less issue the hospital has to worry about," Camille said when she and Maxwell were in the elevator.

"Unless the signed DNR is missing," Maxwell reminded her. "If Terrence or someone else misplaced the document, there could still be legal ramifications."

"Let's hope not," she said.

Maxwell escorted her to her office, then left to go to the one he was using.

"I spoke with the event coordinator this afternoon," her assistant announced. "The Beacon Lighting Company is confirmed."

"Great," Camille said with a smile. She was relieved that everything was going well with the planning for the charity ball. It was an important night for Hopewell General.

The telephone rang, interrupting their conversation.

"Why don't you get some lunch?" Camille suggested

to her assistant before she picked up the phone. "We'll finish up this afternoon."

Lori replied, "Thanks. I won't be gone long."

Camille walked into her office and answered her phone on the fourth ring. "Camille Hunter speaking."

Hearing Maxwell's voice on the other end of the phone brought a smile to her lips. "I was just thinking about you."

"I didn't get a chance to tell you how much I love you," he said.

"I really don't think I'll ever get tired of hearing it," she responded. "I love you, too."

"This weekend meant a whole lot to me, Camille," Maxwell stated. "I want you to know that."

She smiled. "It holds a lot of meaning for me as well."

"So you don't have any regrets?" Maxwell asked.

"I don't," she replied. "I gave myself to the man I love. I can't regret something so special. No man has ever made me feel the way you make me feel," Camille confessed. "It's like we have this special connection. I don't think anyone understands me the way that you do." She switched the phone from one ear to the other.

"You're right," Maxwell interjected. "We do have a connection. You and I…we're tied to each other emotionally."

She smiled. "I love talking to you and, as much as I don't want this conversation to end, I'd better get off this phone so that I can get some work done."

"I have to go over some documents before tomorrow," he responded. "But I'd rather continue our conversation."

"I hope that we will always have times like this," Camille stated. "Where we just talk. Communication is very important to me."

"Camille, I promise you that we will. We'll always have moments like this. I love you more than I can put into words. As you know, I am rarely without something to say."

She laughed.

They said their goodbyes and ended the call.

Camille remained seated for a moment, her eyes closed as she imagined Maxwell in the room with her, silent declarations of love shining brightly in his eyes.

Chapter 13

There were times when Camille didn't quite know what to make of Maxwell Wade. He just seemed too good to be true. But then again, she really didn't have a lot of experience to go on, since she had never really been involved in a serious relationship.

He had flowers delivered to her shortly after lunch. She inhaled the sweet scent of the roses and smiled all afternoon.

It was almost five-thirty when the man himself came looking for her.

Camille's blood coursed through her veins like an awakened river when Maxwell took her by the hand and said, "Time to go home."

When they were in the car, Camille turned to him, asking, "Why are being so good to me, Maxwell?"

He laughed. "Why not? You're the woman I love and I think you deserve to be pampered."

"I'm not complaining," Camille said. "Don't get me wrong. It's all new to me, but I'm loving it."

Maxwell smiled. "Good. I like spoiling you."

"But every now and then, you're going to have to let me spoil you, too."

He glanced over at her. "Really?"

No woman ever wanted to spoil him—they were too busy on the receiving end. Camille was genuine and very caring. He had witnessed her in the hospital, talking to the patients or playing with children. She loved people in general, a quality that was a complement to her job.

Maxwell drove to her townhome and parked the rental car.

Camille looped her arm through his. "So who's doing the cooking tonight?"

He cocked his head to the side, thinking for a moment. "I think we should both do it."

She looked up at him and grinned. "Honey, I'm just messing with you. I will do the cooking. You sit down and relax."

They walked inside, hand in hand.

Camille went upstairs and changed clothes. When she came down, Maxwell was coming out of the guest bathroom. He had changed as well.

"You're sure you don't want me to help cook dinner?"

Camille shook her head. "I'll be fine. I'm just going to make something quick and easy."

While he watched TV, she cooked a pot of angel hair pasta. Camille pulled out a freezer bag containing leftover grilled chicken, and another with shrimp. She heated them in a skillet, leaving them to prepare an Alfredo sauce.

Twenty minutes later, dinner was ready and they sat down to eat.

"My mom told me to tell you hello," Maxwell stated. "I talked to her right before we left the hospital."

"Your parents are very sweet," she said. "I really liked them."

"They liked you, too. Especially my mother." Maxwell gave a short chuckle. "This is a big deal because she has never once liked anyone I've dated."

Camille smiled. "I'm honored."

While they ate, they discussed their day at the hospital.

"How are things going with the lawsuit?" Camille asked. "We've gotten a few requests to confirm or deny some of the allegations made by Terrence and his family."

"What are you telling them?" he asked.

"We haven't responded to their calls."

"Good," Maxwell stated. "At this point, that is probably the best course of action. Hopewell General does not need to comment."

"I really liked Terrence," Camille said. "I've been tempted to call him just to say hello, but I don't think I should at this point."

"Right now it may be best to keep your distance," Maxwell warned. "You don't want to be dragged into the middle of this, sweetheart."

Camille nodded in agreement.

After dinner they sat down in the living room to watch a movie.

Exhausted, Camille was grateful to finally sit down and relax. She fell asleep with her head on Maxwell's chest.

He wrapped his arms around her, holding her close to his heart.

Camille slept soundly for an hour.

Maxwell was still watching television with the volume turned down low when she woke up.

"Hey, beautiful."

Heat rushed to her face. "I'm so sorry, Maxwell. I didn't mean to fall asleep on you like that. I had no idea I was so tired."

"I hope you feel rested."

"I do," Camille confirmed, running her fingers through her hair. "I really needed that nap. I was tired."

She stood up and stretched.

Maxwell turned off the television. "Now that you've gotten your nap out of the way, why don't we go out for dessert?" he suggested.

"Do you really want to go out?" she asked.

He could tell from her expression that Camille preferred to stay home. "We don't have to go out if you're not up for it."

"I'd rather not."

"So what would you like to do?" he asked her.

Camille pulled out two controllers.

Maxwell was surprised. "You actually want to play video games?"

Grinning, she nodded. "I saw your video game consoles in your media room. Why didn't you tell me you liked playing?"

He shrugged. "It was just something I would do to pass the time. Kendra hated them. She would tell me that video games were for kids."

"She's wrong," Camille stated bluntly. "I love playing—it's a way to relieve stress for me. I'm glad that you play."

"Okay. Well, I hope you're not a sore loser," he told her.

She tossed him a controller. "Show me what you got."

They sat down in competition mode.

Maxwell won the first game, much to Camille's dismay. She wasn't a sore loser, but she would've preferred getting the first win. Camille had a feeling that Maxwell was not going to ever let her forget it.

She screamed, and then jumped up and down when she won the second one.

"Okay," Maxwell uttered. "It was a lucky shot, just so you know."

"Whatever."

Maxwell groaned when Camille won again.

She burst in laughter. "I can't hear you."

"I'm not sure if I like this competitive side of you," Maxwell teased. "Your arrogance is showing."

Camille broke into a short laugh. "Honey, you're just not used to losing."

He had to admit that Camille had a point. Maxwell had only lost two cases in his career.

They played until the clock struck midnight.

"Do you want to just stay here?" she asked him.

Maxwell nodded. "Sure."

They turned off the game and headed to Camille's bedroom.

In bed, they held each other as they talked.

Camille traced the outline of his face with her fingers. "I still have a hard time believing that I have someone as wonderful as you in my life."

Maxwell gave her a sexy grin. "I feel the same way about you."

She pulled his face down to hers. "I have never really been in love until I met you."

They shared a kiss.

His kisses sparked a flame of passion, sending spirals of ecstasy through Camille. In no time she and Maxwell were united in a lover's dance under the glow of moonlight.

She couldn't imagine ever tiring of him.

Satisfied, they lay together beneath rumpled sheets, still holding on to each other.

The next day, Thomas Bradshaw stopped by Maxwell's office.

"Lia and I are having a dinner party on Thursday. We'd like for you and Camille to join us. Jaclyn and Lucien will be there as well."

"I'll get with Camille and see if she has any plans," he told his friend. "I'll give you a call."

They talked about the lawsuit for a moment, and then Thomas left to check in on his patients before leaving for the day.

Maxwell went back through the stack of witness statements concerning Terrence Matthews. He reached for the telephone and placed a call to the former doctor's attorney. He was intent on getting the lawsuit settled before the New Year.

Terrence didn't have a legal leg to stand on, despite what he had been told by his attorney. He had been caught red-handed stealing drugs. That by itself was a criminal act, despite his family trying to drag the hospital's name through the mud.

It was time to bring the lawsuit to an end.

Maxwell walked out of his office, bumping into Camille.

She pulled the folds of her sweater together. "Hey…"

"Hey yourself. Where are you going?"

"I thought I'd go downstairs and just walk around

for a bit," she told him. "I need to get out of my office for a few minutes."

"Cold?"

Camille nodded. "It's a little chilly in here, but I'll be fine. The walk will warm me up."

"Thomas and Lia are hosting a dinner party on Thursday night and they invited us," he said. "Are you interested in attending?"

She looked up at him. "Sure. I'd like to go."

Maxwell decided to walk with Camille as she made rounds to the pediatric wing.

"You're wonderful with the children," he told her.

Grinning, she responded, "I love kids."

"How many do you want?" Maxwell inquired. Kendra never wanted children, so he had never thought much about becoming a father until now.

She smiled. "Maybe two. I'd like a little boy and a girl."

He was little surprised that she did not probe any further. He asked the question and she simply answered him. If she was curious about him wanting children, Camille didn't show it.

Camille stopped to chat with a young boy.

"Hello, friend," she said.

"Hey, freen," he responded with a huge grin. "I been looking for you. I thought you was going to come see me this morning."

"I'm sorry, Billy. I had a lot of work to do this morning, so I couldn't come see you until now. How are you doing?"

"I hurt," he said softly.

Maxwell watched as Camille rubbed the little boy's back. "I'm so sorry that you're in pain. Did you tell the nurse?"

"Mama did."

A woman walked over to them.

"Mrs. Johnson," Camille greeted. "It's good to see you."

Maxwell noted the dark circles beneath her eyes and the way the woman's clothes hung on her thin frame. Her son's illness had affected her greatly and his heart went out to her.

When he and Camille were out of the woman's hearing, Maxwell asked, "What's wrong with the little boy?"

"He has leukemia."

Maxwell's heart dropped. "I'm sorry to hear that."

Camille agreed. "Billy is such a sweetie. All of the kids here in the hospital are darlings. It breaks my heart when they have bad days. I have this idea that it would be nice to have all of the rooms in the peds wing equipped with video games. It won't stop the pain, but it could help pass the time for them."

He considered her idea. "I think that's a great idea, Camille."

"We don't have the funding for something like that. Right now, our focus is on the new cancer center."

They took the elevator back up to the second floor.

Maxwell escorted Camille to her office. "I'll call Thomas and confirm that we're attending the dinner party."

She smiled. "I'll see you later."

He blew her a kiss, and then turned around to head back to his office. The more time he spent with Camille, the more he loved her.

Camille was glad that she and Maxwell attended the dinner party. It had given her a chance to get to know

Lia. She had also fallen in love with Thomas and Lia's little boy Jalen.

"I see that I'm not the only one who loves children," she told Maxwell on the way home.

"I'd like to have children one day," he blurted out.

Surprised, Camille looked over at him. "Really?"

"Hey, why do you look so surprised?" asked Maxwell.

Shrugging, she responded, "I just never really considered you father material."

It was Maxwell's turn to be surprised. "Why not?"

"I just figured you were a bachelor for life. At least that's how you've been portrayed by the media."

"At one time I would've agreed with you, sweetheart. But now, a lot has changed—most of it has to do with you." He stole a glance at her. "You bring out the best in me."

Camille was touched by his words.

"You know, I'm still trying to get used to Thomas being married and the father of a son," Maxwell said. "Now they are expecting baby number two."

Thomas and Lia had made the announcement that they were pregnant during their dinner party.

"I think it's wonderful," Camille murmured. "They are such a beautiful couple."

Maxwell agreed. "Lia has made Thomas very happy."

"She makes him happy, too," she contributed. "He seems like a totally different man since meeting her."

He pulled up to her town house and parked his car.

"I feel like a new man now that I have you in my life," Maxwell confessed. "Kendra had soured me on relationships."

"If you're relationship with her was so tumultuous, why did you two keep getting back together?"

"I guess because it was familiar," Maxwell responded. "Kendra has her own money. I never worried that she only wanted me for financial security."

Camille was surprised. "Do you think that's all you have to offer a woman?"

"No," he said. "But you'd be amazed at how many women I meet who only see dollar signs when it comes to me."

"It's their loss, Maxwell. You are so much more."

He wowed her with his smile. "You're a very special woman, Camille. I am honored to have you in my life."

Camille unlocked her door. She turned around, facing him. "Show me."

They were in each other's arms the moment she and Maxwell walked inside the town house, their desire insatiable.

The following Saturday, Camille and Maxwell drove down to Richmond, Virginia, to visit with her parents. This was the first time they would be meeting someone she was dating.

"So your parents have never met any of your boyfriends?" Maxwell asked.

She glanced over at him. "I didn't have a lot of boyfriends and the ones I did have were not worth taking home."

"I'm surprised you didn't have a trail of boys following you around."

Camille chuckled. "I played sports. I didn't have time for boys, really. My parents kept me busy with basketball, tennis and even softball. When I wasn't playing a sport, I was studying. I didn't really start dating until I went to college." She made a face. "Mostly a complete waste of time."

"I have never met a woman as fascinating as you."

"Maxwell, there is nothing fascinating about me," Camille countered.

"Most women I've come in contact with are girly girls. They are more concerned with breaking a nail or the latest fashions than playing sports. If I never endure another fashion week, it will be too soon."

She burst into laughter.

Camille's mother opened the front door as soon as they stepped on the porch.

"Come on in," she told them. "Come in out of the cold."

"Mama, this is Maxwell," Camille said, introducing them. "This is Sarah Hunter, my mother."

"It's a pleasure to meet you, Mrs. Hunter."

Sarah embraced Maxwell. "It's so nice to meet you, too. Camille mentioned that you are working with the hospital on a case."

"Yes, ma'am."

She smiled at her daughter, barely concealing her excitement. Camille's mother had been after her for years to find a nice man to settle down with.

Camille took Maxwell by the hand. "I'm going to show him to his room. I'll be back down in a few minutes."

"Okay, sweetie," Sarah responded. "Your father should be home soon. He ran out to pick up a few things from the grocery store."

Upstairs, Maxwell turned to Camille and said, "Your mother is a sweetheart."

She nodded in agreement. "We have always been close."

"Let's hope that I can pass the test with your father."

Camille laughed. "I guess we'll just have to see."

Her father arrived just as she and Maxwell were on their way downstairs to join her mother.

She ran the rest of the way down. "Dad, I want you to meet someone."

Maxwell joined them at the bottom of the stairs.

Her father eyed him critically for a moment before saying, "Maxwell Wade, welcome to my home." He looked over at his daughter and said, "You didn't tell me that you were dating Maxwell Wade."

Camille stared into green eyes that matched her own. "It just never really came up."

Sarah and Camille were in the kitchen preparing lunch while Maxwell sat with her father in the family room, watching a basketball game.

"He's very handsome," her mother whispered. "I can't believe that you're dating the Maxwell Wade."

Camille smiled. "I think he's handsome, too," she whispered back. "He's not just *the* Maxwell Wade, Mama. He is the man that I love."

"Does he feel the same way about you?"

She nodded.

Sarah embraced her daughter. "I'm so happy for you, Camille."

Her sister Sharon arrived within the hour.

"Where's the munchkin?" Camille asked, referring to her five-year-old nephew.

"With his dad," Sharon responded with a chuckle. "They are doing the male-bonding thing."

"Oh, I was looking forward to seeing him," Camille stated.

"Paul's going to bring him over here around four," Sharon said. "So where is this mystery guy you're dating?" she asked.

"He's with dad," Camille responded. "They were in

the family room, but they may be in the basement or upstairs somewhere."

"Can I tell her?" her mother asked. She was bubbling over with excitement. Camille assumed that it was because she had feared that her youngest daughter would end up an old maid.

"Sure, Mama."

Puzzled, Sharon looked from one to the other. "Tell me what?"

"Camille is dating Maxwell Wade," Sarah announced proudly.

Her sister's eyes widened in her shock. *"Seriously?"*

"Yes," Camille confirmed.

"You go, girl," Sharon said. "That is one fine man."

"He sure is," their mother interjected, surprising them both.

She looked at her daughters. "What? I'm married—not dead."

Ten minutes later, everyone was seated at tables dining on salmon, a Caesar salad and zucchini bread.

"Mama outdid herself," Sharon whispered to her. "I still can't get my salmon to come out like this."

Camille agreed. She sliced off a piece of the tender fish and stuck it into her mouth, savoring the flavor. "Mama's not going to give up her recipe, either."

Maxwell sampled the fish, chewing thoughtfully with his eyes closed. "There's a hint of sweetness," he said.

Opening his eyes, Maxwell asked Sarah, "Did you use syrup?"

Surprised, Sarah nodded. "How did you know, Maxwell?"

"It's what I use when I cook mine," he responded with a smile. "I use that and a raspberry vinaigrette."

Sharon wiped her mouth with her napkin. "You cook?"

Before he could respond, Camille interjected, "He's a wonderful cook."

Her sister smiled in approval. "I keep threatening to send my husband over here for cooking lessons. That man can't make toast without burning it."

They all laughed.

After lunch, they all settled in the family room.

"You are glowing, Camille," her sister told her. "I'm glad to see you so happy."

"I'm very happy," Camille confirmed.

"What about that ex-girlfriend of his?" Sharon asked. "Do you have to deal with her?"

She shook her head no. "She and Maxwell are over for good."

Camille stole a peek at him. Maxwell was in a deep conversation with her father about some NBA player. It thrilled her to see them interacting.

Everything was perfect.

Camille's brother-in-law, Paul, and her nephew arrived shortly after four. Her heart overflowed with joy as she watched Maxwell interact with Paul Jr. He was wonderful with kids.

They left for the restaurant at six to have dinner. Maxwell insisted on picking up the tab, but her father refused.

Her family approved of Maxwell, which meant a great deal to Camille. She was very close to her parents and her sister. She'd wanted Maxwell to get to know them since he was now an important part of her life.

So important that she regretted they would not be sharing the same bed tonight. Out of respect for her parents Maxwell would be staying in her sister's old room.

She was going to miss waking up beside the man she loved.

Camille felt him watching her. She met his gaze.

He smiled and winked at her, setting her heart aflutter.

Later that evening after Sharon and her family left, Camille and Maxwell were still up talking. Her parents had retired to their bedroom almost an hour ago.

"So what do you think of my family?" she asked in a low whisper.

"Your parents are nice," Maxwell told her. "Your sister is something else. She reminds me of mine." He chuckled softly. "That nephew of yours is quite a handful."

Camille agreed and then said, "Maxwell, they all really liked you. I think my mother was a bit starstruck."

He laughed. "I did notice that your father kept eyeing me. I guess he wanted to make sure that I have good intentions toward you. I almost asked his permission to date you."

Camille laughed. "He can be a bit intimidating at times, but you have nothing to worry about. If he didn't like you, he would have made it abundantly clear to me. He has always been very protective of his daughters."

"I'm glad," he responded, stroking her cheek. "I love you, and having your parents' blessings will certainly make things easier."

"I feel the same way about your parents."

Maxwell hugged her. "I love the way you feel in my arms. I don't know how much sleep I'm going to get tonight with you down the hall from me."

She grinned. "It's only for tonight."

"I have a feeling that it's going to be a long night," he said in a loud whisper.

They laughed.

Camille and Maxwell went upstairs shortly after 1:00 a.m.

He kissed her outside the door of her old bedroom.

She showered and slipped on a T-shirt and a pair of sweats, then climbed into bed, propping up the pillows behind her. She was already missing Maxwell.

Camille decided to do some reading before she fell asleep. Hopefully, it would take her mind off of Maxwell and the fact that he was sleeping nearby.

She briefly considered sneaking down to his room, but changed her mind. Camille didn't want to take advantage of the trust her parents placed in her.

Her cell phone rang.

It was Maxwell.

"I guess you're having a hard time falling asleep, too," she said when she answered the call.

He gave a short laugh. "I figured we could continue our conversation until we get sleepy."

They talked for the next hour. Her eyelids grew heavy and she started yawning. Good night, sweetheart," Maxwell told her. "I'll see you in a few hours."

"See you soon."

Six hours later, Camille went downstairs to help her mother prepare breakfast.

"It felt good being back in my old room," she stated.

Sarah smiled. "I'm glad. I hope Maxwell slept well."

Camille peeked into the oven. "You're making your homemade blueberry muffins?"

"I sure am," her mother confirmed. "I know how much you love them."

"I miss your cooking."

"You're a good cook, Camille."

"Thanks, but it's not the same, Mama. Your cooking

reminds me of home and all of the happy memories we've made here in this house."

Sarah nodded in agreement. "I used to feel the same way about my mother's cooking. But then I had a family of my own."

Maxwell came downstairs and entered the kitchen. "Good morning, everyone."

"Good morning," Sarah responded in greeting. "Breakfast is almost ready."

Fifteen minutes later, they all sat down in the dining room to eat.

Camille and Maxwell were planning to leave in a couple of hours. They planned to attend church with her family first.

She was so glad she'd brought Maxwell home to meet her mom and dad because he meant so much a lot to her. Camille wasn't sure where their relationship was heading, but they were becoming closer and closer. When they weren't working, she and Maxwell enjoyed spending time together.

She didn't like to think about the day Maxwell would return to New York permanently. Camille was still unsure about a long-distance relationship, but one thing was certain—she didn't want to lose Maxwell.

Chapter 14

The following week was busy with meetings for Maxwell, and for Camille, placing the final touches on the program for the charity ball.

After the trip to Richmond, Maxwell and Camille decided to spend most of their weekends in New York. They left Friday after work and returned early Monday morning.

This trip, Maxwell took Camille to see a play on Broadway. He had even surprised her with a gorgeous dress to wear. She initially refused the gift when she saw the name of the designer on the label. Camille thought it was too extravagant, but Maxwell insisted she keep it and wear it for their evening on the town.

They returned to the penthouse afterward.

"It's so cold out there," she told Maxwell. "I don't know how you handle this weather."

"It does take getting used to," he said with a short laugh.

"I thought it was really cold in Alexandria, but New York is much, much colder."

Maxwell wrapped his arms around her. "It's a good thing you have me to keep you all nice and warm."

Camille smiled. "Yes, it is."

She laid her head on his chest, listening to the steady rhythm of his heartbeat.

"Ready for bed?" he asked.

Camille glanced up at him. "Sure."

Smiling, Maxwell took her by the hand and led her to the bedroom.

She was surprised to see the rose petals scattered on the bed. A table laden with chocolate-covered strawberries and chilled champagne had been placed in the room. "When did you do this?"

"I had the housekeeper take care of it while we were out," he explained. "This is part of our date. It doesn't end just because we are here."

She smiled. "You're spoiling me, Maxwell."

"You deserve it, Camille."

Her eyes traveled the room. "I love all of this, but I want you to know something. You don't have to buy me expensive gifts. I'm a simple girl. I don't need a lot."

"This is exactly why I enjoy buying you nice things," he responded. "You're my woman. I want to spend money on you. Hey, I can't take it with me."

Camille pulled his face to hers. She kissed him gently on the lips. "You in my life is all I need."

Maxwell picked up a remote.

Soft music began playing in the background.

He turned back to Camille and said, "The rest of the night is just for us."

* * *

Maxwell had fallen hard for Camille. They were in such a good place that it was hard for him to consider leaving her behind when his work for Hopewell General was done.

They walked into the hospital, having driven straight from the airport Monday morning.

Camille rushed off to her office because she had a meeting scheduled in about an hour and she wanted to go over her notes beforehand.

She walked briskly through the doors, waved at her assistant, then sat down at her desk.

"Hey, jet-setter," Jerome teased from the doorway.

Camille smiled. "Good morning, Jerome. What are you doing here so early?"

"I'm working a double," he explained as he took a seat. "Hey, I saw Terrence over the weekend."

Her face registered her surprise. "You did?"

Jerome nodded. "We didn't really talk, though. He acknowledged me and kept moving."

"How did he look?" Camille missed her friend, but with the lawsuit still pending, she had to keep her distance.

"Okay," he responded. "He's lost some weight."

"I've thought about giving him a call, but Maxwell didn't think it was a good idea," Camille said. "I miss him, though."

Jerome shrugged in nonchalance.

She knew that Jerome and Terrence never really got along. They were cordial most times at the hospital. There were a few times when they disagreed over the care of a patient.

"Maybe you should have reached out to him," she suggested.

Jerome looked at her as if she'd grown three heads. "What Terrence needs now is a friend."

"That's not me," Jerome stated flatly. "Rehab is what that boy needs."

Camille sighed softly. "You shouldn't be that way."

He shrugged in nonchalance.

When Jerome left her office, Camille sat at her desk for a moment, debating whether or not she should try and call Terrence. Despite what he had done, all of his friends should not abandon him. He had been sick. This was the reason why he stole the drugs—it was his addiction.

Camille vowed that she wouldn't abandon Terrence.

However, she didn't feel the time was right for her to try and connect with him. Perhaps after the lawsuit was over.

That evening after work, Camille made spaghetti for dinner. Maxwell had a late meeting, but came over straight from the hospital about an hour after Camille.

She and Maxwell sat down to eat.

"How are things going with the fundraiser?" he asked.

"Great," Camille responded. "We almost have everything finalized as far as the menu goes. The auction items are set and a few more are coming in tomorrow."

She wiped her mouth with her napkin. "I have to admit that I'll be thrilled when this event is over."

"Only to do it all over again next year," Maxwell contributed.

Camille chuckled. "Yeah."

After dinner, they decorated her Christmas tree.

"I think we did a fabulous job," she told Maxwell when they finished.

He agreed.

As they admired their work, the telephone rang.

Camille checked the caller ID. "I need to take this," she told him. "It's the event coordinator."

While Camille was on the phone, Maxwell decided to clean up the kitchen for her. She joined him when she was done with her conversation.

"Everything okay?" he asked.

She nodded. "We had a minor glitch, but it's been resolved." Camille embraced him. "Thanks for cleaning up."

"Thanks for making dinner," he responded.

Maxwell placed his lips to hers.

He suddenly picked her up and carried her upstairs to the bedroom where he undressed her slowly and between kisses. Then, taking his time, he made love to her.

Throughout the night, Camille rode the wave of sleeplessness back and forth. She kept waking up every hour, it seemed.

She gave up on sleep shortly after 5:00 a.m. She eased out of bed, put on her robe, and padded barefoot across the floor.

When she peered out of the window, she smiled. It had snowed during the night.

"What are you smiling about?" Maxwell asked, joining her at the window.

"Just thinking about how beautiful it looks outside with fresh snow on the ground. I really hope that we have a white Christmas this year."

He wrapped his arms around her. "You're up early."

"I couldn't sleep."

"Is anything wrong?" he asked, his voice filled with concern.

Camille shook her head. "No." She turned around in his arms. "Everything is perfect, Maxwell."

He kissed her on the forehead. "I hope you will always feel this way."

"Let's go back to bed," she suggested. "I'm not planning to go into the office until ten."

Maxwell grinned in response.

"Maxwell's mom will be here in a couple of hours," Camille announced to Jerome as they entered her town house. He had come over earlier in the day to play a game of basketball. Jerome was also going to house-sit for her until the electrician came by to check out the wiring in her guest room.

"I need to shower and change before Maxwell arrives. He wants to get to the airport early enough for us to park and meet her in the baggage claim area."

Jerome followed her into the bedroom. "You two get along well, so why are you so nervous?"

"Because… I don't know. She's Maxwell's mom," Camille said. "Maybe she was just being nice before."

"Stop trying to find reasons to worry," Jerome stated. "Besides, Maxwell doesn't seem the type to need his mama's permission."

Camille laughed. "No, I guess he isn't."

"So you have nothing to worry about."

"You're right, Jerome."

"I'm going back downstairs so that you can take care of your business."

When Camille was alone, she removed her clothes, walked briskly into the bathroom and turned on the shower. She stepped inside, relishing the feel of the hot water against her skin.

Why am I so nervous about seeing Maxwell's mother again?

Maybe Jerome was right. She was looking for some type of imperfection in their relationship. Camille had never felt such intense emotions before, and she was afraid that something was going to threaten what they had together.

His mother was coming to Alexandria to visit an old friend, but she wanted to have dinner with Maxwell and Camille later that evening. Constance Wade shared similar qualities with her son, one of them being that she was extremely outspoken.

A few minutes later, Camille got out and dried off her body with a towel. She slipped on her robe before padding barefoot into her bedroom.

When she was dressed, Camille went downstairs to join Jerome in the living room.

"You look a lot calmer now."

"I feel much better after my shower," she told Jerome. Checking her watch, she said, "Maxwell should be here shortly."

She ran her fingers through her damp hair to fluff up the natural curls. Camille retrieved a pair of black leather boots from the closet downstairs.

She sat down on the sofa beside Jerome and stepped into her boots.

"I appreciate your staying here until the electrician comes by. What are your plans for this evening?" she asked.

"Julie and I are going to see Prince perform. He's going to be in D.C. tonight."

Camille glanced over at him. "I didn't know that."

"That's because you've been so busy working on the

charity ball, going back and forth to New York," Jerome told her.

"You and Julie have been glued at the hip," Camille stated. 'I guess we're going to have to double date just so that we can spend some time together."

He laughed. "You're probably right."

The doorbell rang.

Camille did a quick check of her reflection in the wall mirror hanging in the foyer before opening the door to let Maxwell inside.

"I'm ready," she told him.

"Hello, Maxwell," Jerome called out.

He responded in kind.

Camille grabbed her coat and purse. "Thanks again for hanging out here. The electrician should be here shortly. Oh, and tape the game for me, Jerome. I'll watch it sometime tonight."

She and Maxwell left the town house.

He had sent the jet for his mother. By the time Maxwell made it to the airport, the plane had landed and his mother was waiting for him inside the terminal.

She hugged Camille, and then her son.

"It's so nice to see you again," Camille told her.

Constance insisted on taking them to lunch.

Maxwell glanced over at Camille, who nodded in approval. She wasn't about to do anything to offend his mother.

Words couldn't describe what Maxwell was feeling at the moment. He was surrounded by the two most important women in his life—his mother and Camille. The two had hit it off immediately and were fast becoming friends.

He smiled as he listened to them chat about shopping

and where to find the best sales. "I've already got all of my Christmas shopping done," his mother was saying. "This is the first year I'm actually looking forward to Christmas."

Maxwell glanced over at Camille, taking her hand in his. "I have so much to be thankful for this year. I've been blessed to have this incredible and beautiful woman in my life."

His mother nodded in agreement. "I'm thrilled for you both," she said.

After lunch, Maxwell and Camille dropped her off at her friend's house, and then drove back to her town-home. She didn't see Jerome's car.

"I guess the electrician has come and gone," Camille commented.

"So does that mean that we have the place all to our-selves?" Maxwell asked, a lusty gleam in his eyes.

She nodded.

Laughing, they rushed into the house.

Maxwell's telephone started to ring.

"It's Ray," he announced. "I'd better get this."

Camille sat down on the edge of her bed.

When he hung up, Maxwell said, "Honey, I have to go. Matthews's attorney just called. Ray and I have a meeting with him in an hour."

"I hope that it goes well," she said.

"Hopefully, I'll have some good news for the hospi-tal," he said as he kissed her goodbye.

Maxwell was ready to play hardball when he walked into the conference room, where Terrence Matthew's attorney was seated at the head of the table. He and Ray sat on opposite sides of the table, facing one another. Maxwell decided to strike first.

"I hope you called this meeting to tell us that your

client has decided not to go forth with this ridiculous lawsuit. Dr. Matthews has a serious drug problem and we can prove it. Our investigators have found some interesting information. This not the first time the doc has been in trouble for stealing drugs." Maxwell had received a report showing that Terrence was arrested when he was fifteen for stealing drugs from a pharmacy.

The attorney struggled to keep his composure. "He was a juvenile and his records were sealed. How did you…" He shook his head.

"Money can only keep a person quiet for so long," Maxwell commented as he leaned forward. "The hospital doesn't want to ruin Terrence Matthews. He needs help—help that they offered to provide, but your client turned down. They could press charges and will be forced to do so, if your client plans to continue this farce."

Maxwell had played the hospital's trump card and believed it would pay off. "The good doctor will lose his medical license and also serve jail time. We have proof that he's been stealing drugs for months. We have the evidence."

The room erupted into thick, tense silence.

It took seconds to conference Terrence and his parents in on a phone call. It was long past time for this lawsuit to come to an end. Dudley never planned to press charges, but the Matthews family did not know that. The hospital had been blindsided when they decided to withdraw their support, but Maxwell wasn't fazed by their money.

He was prepared to prove Terrence's longtime history of drug use, and force Dudley's hand in filing formal charges against the doctor.

The meeting ended. Ray and Maxwell waited until they reached the car before discussing what took place during the conference call.

"You know Dudley would never have pressed charges against Terrence," Ray stated. "That was a bold move, bluffing like that."

Maxwell opened the driver's-side door. "It wasn't a bluff," he responded. "If parading his drug history wasn't enough to end the lawsuit, we were going to have him formally charged and arrested."

Camille paced back and forth nervously across the floor while Maxwell was gone. She couldn't imagine why they would be meeting with the Matthew's attorney, but Camille prayed it was good news. She hoped that a settlement of some kind could be reached to put an end to the litigation. It would be perfect timing since the charity ball was only days away.

Two hours passed before he returned.

Camille met him at the door. "How did it go?" she asked.

He broke into a smile. "It went well. The Matthews family finally admitted that Terrence has a drug problem and is currently seeking treatment. They have also pledged their financial support to Hopewell General."

Camille couldn't believe what she was hearing. "Really?"

"They are not giving as much as they have in the past, but they do not intend to pull out completely."

She shrugged. "Anything is better than nothing. Besides, we recently acquired a new benefactor."

"That's great," Maxwell said.

"Life just keeps getting better and better," Camille said, following him into the living room. "Dr. Dudley is going to be relieved that this is over."

Maxwell sat down on the sofa. "He is. Ray called him after we left the meeting."

"Honey, this is great," Camille responded. "Maybe now we can get back to normal at the hospital." Then her smile disappeared. "This means that you'll be leaving for New York permanently."

"But it doesn't mean that this is the end of us," he assured her.

"I know. It's just that you won't be here working down the hall from me."

Maxwell wrapped an arm around her. "You can always move to New York."

His words stunned her. Camille had not considered how they would handle his return to New York. She had been reveling in her newfound joy so much that she hadn't given it much thought. However, the reality was that their relationship would soon become a long-distance one.

"Camille..." he prompted.

She turned to face him. "I would have to really think about it, Maxwell."

"Does that mean that you're leaning toward relocating?"

Camille didn't want to disappoint him, but she had to be honest. "I don't know. It's a lot to consider."

"It's not something you have to decide right now," Maxwell told her. "I just want you to consider it. I don't want to leave you behind."

Camille smiled at him. "I'll think about it, Maxwell. I'll give it some serious thought."

Maxwell left to take care of some paperwork.

After he'd gone an idea struck Camille, bringing a smile to her face.

Chapter 15

Maxwell strolled into the house and found rose petals strewn on the floor and up the spiral staircase.

His lips turned upward into a smile.

"Honey, I'm home," he called out as he slowly made his way up the stairs.

In the master bedroom, Maxwell found Camille wearing lingerie. She had set up a small table in the master bedroom covered with champagne, two plates laden with lobster, a Caesar salad and rolls. Maxwell noted there was also a silver tray with chocolate-covered strawberries.

"What did I do to deserve this?" he asked with a smile.

"We're celebrating the successful way that you've handled the Matthews lawsuit."

Maxwell kissed her.

"Thank you, sweetheart. I really appreciate this. No one has ever done anything like this for me."

Looking lovingly in his eyes, Camille said, "You deserve this and more." She led him over to the table. "I hope you brought your appetite with you."

They sat down and enjoyed their dinner.

"This was delicious," Maxwell stated. He wiped his mouth with the end of his napkin. "I guess the chocolate-covered strawberries are dessert."

Camille shook her head. "Actually, I had something else in mind."

She stood up, walked to the center of the room and began untying her negligee.

Maxwell's breath caught in his throat at the sight of the beautiful woman standing before him. He would never tire of looking at Camille.

It was becoming clearer to him, that he had found his soul mate. She was the other half of him. Maxwell was not going to risk losing her.

He had to find a way to convince Camille to move to New York.

The hospital was buzzing with the news that the lawsuit had been dropped. Maxwell had also been able to quietly settle the other pending lawsuit with the family for the wrong medication. The heavy cloud hanging over Hopewell General Hospital had finally disappeared.

Maxwell was hailed a hero by many of the staff, including Dr. Dudley.

Camille and her staff were busy handling media requests and working on a press release for the hospital.

A knock on Camille's office door drew her attention away from her project.

A grin spread across her face. "Hey."

Maxwell walked briskly into the office, closing the door behind him. "I have to fly to New York tonight. I'll be gone for a couple of days."

He wrapped his arms around her. "I'm sorry for the late notice."

Turning in his arms, Camille lifted her mouth to him, kissing him softly. Unnamable sensations ran through her as his hands traveled down her body. She felt the heat from their closeness and the pit of her began to burn with his touch.

Maxwell gently grasped Camille's hand, his fingers fondling its smoothness. When she looked up at him, her gaze sent currents through him. He lowered his head and kissed her on the forehead. "I wish you could go with me."

"I wish I could go with you, too, but I can't." She felt an odd twinge of disappointment. The last thing Camille wanted was to be apart from Maxwell for two days. It seemed like an eternity.

"I'll be back before you even realize that I'm gone," Maxwell said, as if he could read her thoughts.

"I doubt that," Camille responded. "I miss you already."

They softly touched lips. The kiss was slow and thoughtful. His tongue traced to soft fullness of her lips, sending shivers of desire racing through her veins. Camille gave herself freely to the passion of his kiss.

When they finally parted, she said, "I love you, Maxwell."

"I love you, too, sweetheart."

Maxwell swept her up one more in his arms.

To both Maxwell and Camille, the hug held much more than an embrace.

* * *

While Maxwell was in New York, Camille worked feverishly.

She was pleased that her fundraising efforts, aided in part by some wonderful contacts she'd met through Maxwell, had netted a huge endowment for Hopewell.

Maxwell was returning to Alexandria today and Camille could hardly wait to see him. Although they talked every night, she still missed him dearly.

She had worked late for the past two days, but she planned to leave an hour early in order to properly plan a romantic homecoming for him.

Maxwell showed up on at her door shortly after 8:00 p.m.

Camille stepped back to let him inside the town house.

Leaning into him, she welcomed his warm embrace.

"I'm so glad to see you, sweetheart," he murmured in her hair. "Those were the longest two days of my life."

Camille laughed. "I know what you mean. I kept thinking that there had to be something wrong with my watch." Gesturing toward the love seat, she stated, "Give me a few minutes to set everything up and then we can eat. Dinner is almost ready."

"Take your time, sweetheart. I'm going to take a shower and change clothes. I came straight here from the airport."

She reached out, pulling him into her arms. "I'm so glad that you're back."

He kissed her. "Me, too."

Half an hour later, Camille led Maxwell into the dining room, where he eyed the beautifully decorated table.

Flames flickered from the silver-colored candles,

casting a soft glow on the succulent display of steak, scalloped potatoes, yeast rolls and steaming broccoli.

"Everything looks delicious."

"Thank you."

Camille sat down in the chair Maxwell pulled out for her.

He eased into a chair facing her.

She smiled when Maxwell closed his eyes as she chewed. Camille was pleased to see that he was enjoying his meal. She loved cooking for him. Camille also enjoyed the times when they were together in the kitchen preparing meals. She cherished those special moments. It was something she had seen her parents do, and those shared moments had seemed to draw them closer.

Her parents were not only husband and wife—they were also best friends. Camille had never seen her parents yell or argue. This didn't mean that they always agreed with one another. They were able to talk any problems through. Camille wanted this type of relationship with Maxwell.

After the dessert, Maxwell insisted on helping Camille with cleaning up. When they were done, they retired to the living room.

"You're spoiling me," Maxwell told Camille. "All of this attention. I'm not used to this."

She frowned. "You get a lot of attention, Maxwell. You can't walk into a room without every woman staring you down."

"I'm not talking about that kind of attention. I'm usually the one lavishing my attention on the person I'm dating. It's all about them."

"Then you've been dating the wrong women," she blurted.

He laughed. "I'm sure you're right."

"Maxwell, I want shared memories and experiences between us," Camille stated. "It can't be one hundred percent about me or you."

He agreed.

"In this relationship, we are going to be spoiling each other," she told him. Camille never tired of looking into his gorgeous brown eyes. Tonight they seemed to have a golden glow.

"I enjoyed the thought you placed in preparing dinner," Maxwell stated.

"I'm glad you enjoyed dinner. I wanted to make something nice for your return."

His eyes clung to hers. "Well, you certainly accomplished the task. You made all of my favorites."

Moving closer, she leaned her head on his chest as they watched television.

Three hours later, Maxwell gently sat Camille up and rose to his feet. "You look tired. Let's go to bed."

Camille was tired, but she also ached for his touch. So much that her feelings for him intensified, wrapping around her like a warm, comfortable throw. She led him by the hand to her bedroom. Standing in the middle of the floor, they undressed each other in silence.

Maxwell held her in his arms, his eyes making passionate love to her. "I love you so much, baby."

He swept Camille, weightless, into his arms and carried her to the bed.

After placing her in the middle of the bed, he crawled in behind her.

Camille could feel his uneven breathing on her cheek as he held her close. The touch of his hand was almost unbearable in its tenderness.

His mouth covered hers hungrily, leaving Camille's mouth burning with fire.

The touch of his lips on hers sent a shock wave through her entire body with a familiar intensity. As he planted kisses on her shoulders, neck and face, he roused her passion to a fever pitch.

She drew him closer, eager to touch his skin. As aroused as she was, she was surprised that they took time to explore and give each other pleasure. Then she could wait no more, as passion pounded the blood through her heart, chest and head, causing her to breathe in deep soul-drenching drafts.

She led Maxwell to her and when he entered her she exploded in a powerful climax. In no time, he followed her.

Afterward, Camille lay in his arms, sighing in pleasant exhaustion.

Chapter 16

"Hello, darling," a woman murmured from behind him in the lobby of the hotel.

Maxwell had just arrived at Morrison House and was on his way up to his suite to await Camille's arrival. He stopped by the desk to pick up a package that had been sent to him.

Shocked to the core, he whipped around at the sound of the voice that he found very familiar. "Kendra, what are you doing here?"

He was expecting Camille at any moment. The last thing he needed was for her to show up while Kendra was there. His ex-girlfriend would stage a scene in a heartbeat and he didn't want to subject Camille to her antics.

"I came to see you, silly," she responded with a sexy laugh that was drawing attention to them. "Why else would I take a trip to Virginia?" Kendra glanced around. "How can you stand it here? Is this the best that Alexandria has to offer?"

He grabbed her by the arm and led her over to a corner of the lobby. "I'll repeat the question," Maxwell said. "Why are you here?"

Oblivious to the people milling about in the lobby, watching them, she asked, "You aren't still mad at me, are you?"

He was careful to keep his voice low. "I can't believe you discussed our relationship on that reality show of yours. Kendra, we had an agreement."

"Maxwell, don't be angry," she whined. "I'm still in love with you and so, I made it known to the world. What's wrong with that?"

"And you felt the need to talk about the physical aspects of our relationship as well?"

Kendra eyes traveled from his face downward. "Honey, you have absolutely nothing to be ashamed of, trust me."

"I wish you'd contacted me before coming here," Maxwell said. "If you had, then I would've told you not to waste your time."

She looked at him with pleading eyes. "Maxwell, we love each other and I'm really tired of playing this game. There is not another woman out there that can do for you what I do. You know that."

"Kendra, I assure you that I'm not playing a game," Maxwell told her. "What we had is over. You and I want different things out of life. You wanted a reality show and you've got it. It's made you millions, so why don't you concentrate on that?"

She flipped her long hair over her shoulder. "I had money before the show. What I want is to be with you, Maxwell. I know that for sure. We are a power couple—you and I."

Maxwell shook his head. "You want fame and you're willing to do anything to get it. I heard about your new book deal—the one in which you plan to tell all. Seriously, are you really planning to reveal all of your sexual conquests?"

"They were relationships, Maxwell. And why not? I've been involved with some of the world's most famous men. I shouldn't have to keep it a secret."

"I suppose I'll be featured in your book."

She gave him a seductive smile. "It's not like I'm going to say anything negative."

"Kendra, do not mention me in that book or I will have you in court," Maxwell warned.

"Ooh, that sounds like a threat," she said with a laugh.

Maxwell shook his head. "It's a promise."

"Why don't we go to your suite and talk?" Kendra suggested. "We can get reacquainted. Don't you want that?"

"I have plans for the evening," he replied.

Kendra's smile quickly disappeared and her eyes narrowed. "What kind of plans?"

"I don't owe you any explanations, Kendra," Maxwell stated without feeling. "We are no longer seeing each other."

"Is it with Thomas or another woman?" she demanded.

Maxwell gave her a hard stare but didn't respond to her question. "I'm sorry you came all this way, but if you'd called me first, I could have told you not to bother." It was none of her business whether or not he was seeing someone. Maxwell didn't owe her any explanations.

"That's exactly why I didn't tell you," Kendra shot back.

He turned and headed to the elevator. When she tried to follow, Maxwell announced, "I'm going upstairs *alone*."

Maxwell had just entered his suite when Camille called to say she was downstairs.

He met her at the elevator in case Kendra was somewhere lurking. Maxwell didn't want her confronting Camille. He hoped that Kendra was on her way to D.C. by now. She didn't care much for Alexandria and had complained every time they came to visit Thomas.

"Aren't you sweet," Camille said when the elevator doors opened. "You didn't have to meet me at the elevator."

"Hey, I'm your protector. I'm just doing my job to keep my woman safe."

She surveyed Maxwell's face, and then paused a moment before asking, "Is there a problem? You look upset."

"No. Of course not, sweetheart," he said. Maxwell grabbed her hand and led her to his suite.

As soon as Camille entered the suite, Maxwell pulled her into his arms, holding her close.

He kissed her hungrily.

"Wow," she murmured. "Now this is some greeting."

"I couldn't help myself." Maxwell debated whether or not to tell Camille about Kendra being in town. He didn't want to ruin their evening, however, so he made the decision to keep quiet. Hopefully, his ex-girlfriend would just give up and leave him alone.

He and Camille sat down on the sofa.

"I need to finish some Christmas shopping on Saturday," she announced. "Would you like to go with me?"

"You still have to buy presents?" Maxwell asked. "As much shopping as you did in New York, I thought you were finished."

Camille shook her head. "I still have a few more gifts to buy and then I'm done."

Maxwell shook his head. "You said that last week."

She broke into a short laugh. "And it's still true."

Maxwell slipped an arm around her. "You are turning out to be quite a shopper. I think my mother is rubbing off on you."

"I love shopping with her," Camille said. "She has an eye for bargains."

He laughed. "My mom loves her coupons."

Maxwell was relieved when Camille wanted to stay in for the evening. He called and ordered dinner, while she found something on television to watch.

A knock on the door made Maxwell uneasy, which Camille didn't miss. "Are you okay?" she inquired. "You seem jumpy."

He walked briskly to the door.

Maxwell stepped out of the way for the waiter to roll the cart inside. He stuck his head out, scanning the hallway.

I've got to get a hold of myself. Kendra is not the type of woman to stand around in the hallway.

He felt Camille's eyes on him.

Maxwell closed the door, signed the check and tipped the waiter.

They sat down to eat.

"Are you sure everything is okay?" Camille questioned. "You're not acting like yourself, Maxwell."

He saw the concern on her face. "Honey, everything

is fine." He reached over and covered her hand with his own.

She smiled. "I didn't see you much at the hospital today. I heard you were in meetings most of the day with Dr. Dudley."

"Have you started listening to the hospital grapevine?" he asked.

Camille shook her head. "Thomas mentioned it in passing when I was looking for Dr. Dudley."

Maxwell met her gaze. "How is he treating you?"

"Fine," Camille responded. "There is still this air of tension between us, but I'm trying to work through it. He doesn't make the comments he used to make. That helps."

Maxwell had made it clear to Dudley that even after he returned to New York, he and Camille would still continue their relationship. He warned the chief of staff that he would have to answer to him if he was ever out of line with Camille. However, Maxwell was still hoping she would move to New York.

During his last trip to New York, Maxwell found the perfect engagement ring for Camille. He was planning on asking her to marry him and decided that Christmas would be the perfect day to do so. She was the woman for him and Maxwell wanted to spend the rest of his life with her.

They finished eating and sat down on the sofa to watch a movie.

Throughout the movie, she and Maxwell shot furtive glances at each other. Camille knew what he was thinking because it echoed her very own thoughts.

When the movie ended, Maxwell and Camille rose to their feet.

Camille's heart fluttered at his touch. "Why don't we take this into the bedroom?" she suggested seductively.

In response, Maxwell led the way.

Maxwell woke up with a start. He initially thought he had been dreaming, but then he heard it again.

Someone was knocking on his door.

Maxwell glanced over at Camille, who was still sleeping. Apparently, the sound hadn't disturbed her.

He eased out of bed so that he wouldn't awaken Camille and padded barefoot across the floor, wincing at the feel of the cold floor.

"So who is she?" Kendra questioned when he opened his door. She stood there with her hands on her hips and her eyes revealing her anger and jealousy.

"I thought you were gone," Maxwell responded coldly. He didn't even bother to hide his irritation at being disturbed this late at night.

Kendra gave him a little smile. "Baby, I'm not giving up on you that easily. You should know that by now. Now who was the tramp that came to see you? I heard her talking to you on her cell phone. I would've confronted her, but I had to meet someone in D.C."

"Why didn't you stay in D.C.?"

"Because I wanted to be near you, even in this *little* hotel, Maxwell," she responded. "We have some things we need to iron out, don't you think?"

"We're talking in circles," Maxwell stated. "I'm done."

"C'mon, baby," she pleaded. "Please let me in."

He sighed impatiently. "I have long day tomorrow, so please, Kendra, leave."

"Why won't you let me in?" she asked. "Is…is that

tramp still in there? Maxwell, are you sleeping with her?"

"Goodbye, Kendra." Maxwell closed the door, putting an end to her rant.

Maxwell half expected Kendra to knock on the door or cause a scene in the hallway, but was relieved when she didn't. He was also thankful that she didn't have her camera crew with her.

He went back into the bedroom and climbed into bed.

"Who was that?" Camille asked. She sat up, pulling the covers up to cover her nude body. "Whoever she was she wasn't trying to keep her voice down."

She wouldn't look at him and it bothered Maxwell. He wasn't going to lie to Camille, so he decided that it was best to break his silence.

"That was Kendra," Maxwell told her. "She showed up her earlier tonight, and I thought she'd taken my suggestion to go back to New York, but clearly she decided to stay."

"How long has she been in town?" Camille questioned.

He shrugged. "I don't know. She came here uninvited. I want you to know that I had nothing to do with her showing up."

"I believe you," Camille said. "What I don't understand is why you didn't tell me that she was here."

"I didn't want to upset you and I didn't want to put a damper on our evening," he said truthfully.

"Well, one thing's for sure, Maxwell, it didn't sound like she's over you," Camille stated.

Maxwell shrugged. "I've been honest with Kendra. Our relationship is over and it has been for months."

He placed a hand to Camille's face. "I'm in love with someone else."

She smiled.

"I love you, baby."

"I love you too," she murmured.

He pulled her down into the bed. "Show me…"

"You're all aglow," Jerome teased Camille the very next day when she arrived to work.

"I thought you were off today," Camille commented. "What are you doing here?"

"I'm helping to wrap the Christmas presents for the peds wing."

She smiled. "I don't know why you won't just settle down and have a family of your own as much as you love children. Jerome, you would make a wonderful father."

"I have to find my children a wonderful mother— especially since you are no longer on the market."

Camille laughed. "Jerome, you need to quit playing. We're more like brother and sister."

He nodded. "Yeah, because you are too high-maintenance for me."

"Whatever," she uttered.

"I called you last night."

"Did you call my cell?" she asked.

"I called both numbers. I figured you were with Maxwell doing the horizontal tango."

She flushed with embarrassment. "I was with him. Jerome, you wouldn't believe what happened."

"What?" Jerome asked.

"He had a visitor while I was there."

Jerome's eyes widened in his surprise. "Who? Were y'all up there making too much noise?"

Camille folded her arms across her chest. "Jerome, not everything is about sex."

"It isn't? Hey, nobody told me."

"Jerome…"

He laughed. "Okay, sweetie. Who came to see your man?"

"His ex-girlfriend," Camille announced. "Shortly after midnight."

Jerome sat up straight. "Kendra Dixon? That ex-girlfriend?"

Camille nodded.

"Hey, you should've called me," Jerome responded. "I would have gladly taken her off Maxwell's hands. We could've had a party, you know—"

"Focus, Jerome."

"Okay, I'm sorry." He surveyed Camille's face. "How did things go between you all?"

"Maxwell didn't let her inside the suite, but I could hear them talking. Kendra isn't ready to let go of their relationship yet. That much is clear."

"So what does Mr. Wade have to say?"

"He wants to be with me," Camille responded. "I believe him, but I don't think Kendra is going to just disappear out of our lives. They have way too much history for that."

"Well, as long as he's not trying to play you two against each other."

"Maxwell is way too mature for that," she told Jerome. "It's one of the qualities I love about him. He likes to put all of his cards on the table."

"Then what bothers you about this?"

"I don't do drama," Camille said. "You've seen Kendra on the news. She loves attention and it doesn't matter how she gets it. For all I know, she may try and stage a catfight just for her reality show."

"Then you know what to do," Jerome said. "Just whoop that tail on national TV."

Her assistant interrupted them. "You have a message from the caterers," she told Camille. "They want you to call them right away."

Camille released a long sigh. "Please don't let anything be wrong this close to the ball."

Jerome headed to the door. "I'll check in with you later. As for Kendra Dixon, don't lose a minute of sleep over her."

She nodded as she picked up the phone and dialed.

Camille sent up a silent prayer of thanks when she got off the telephone. There was nothing wrong with the menu. The caterer just wanted the final count. Everything was going to be fine.

Life couldn't be more perfect.

Chapter 17

Maxwell and Camille had just returned from lunch when Kendra walked out of one of the hospital rooms with Dr. Dudley.

"I don't believe her," Maxwell muttered. His mouth tightened when Kendra glanced in his direction. She gave him a smug smile, and then leaned over and whispered something in Dudley's ear.

"What is she doing here?" Camille asked Jaclyn, who was standing near the nurse's station, reading a medical chart.

"She's visiting some of the patients."

Maxwell noted the flash of anger in Camille's eyes when she said, "This wasn't cleared through me." He should have anticipated Kendra doing something like this. She would do anything to try and get to him.

"Knowing Kendra, she went straight to Dudley," he told Camille. "I'm sorry. I should have expected something like this."

"She has a camera crew with her," Camille complained. "These patients don't need to be subjected to this type of exposure. Kendra should have coordinated a visit through me so that the proper releases could be signed."

"She won't be able to air any of the footage without signed releases from the patients," Maxwell said. "I'll make sure of that."

Kendra ran her fingers through her curls as she sashayed toward them.

Maxwell held back his temper as he watched Kendra size up Camille from head to toe, instantly viewing her as the competition.

Camille glanced over at him as if waiting for him to say something.

"Why are you doing this?" he asked her in a low voice.

"The patients have all been happy to see me, Maxwell," she replied, a fake smile on her face. "Regardless of what you may think, my visit is good publicity for the hospital. From what I've been reading about Hopewell General, they can use some positive publicity." She glanced over at Camille and said, "Aren't you going to introduce me?"

"Camille, this is Kendra Dixon," Maxwell said. "Camille Hunter is the director of public relations here at the hospital. She's the one you should have spoken to regarding this hospital visit."

Kendra shrugged in response. "Why? Especially when I spoke directly with the chief of staff."

She glanced over at Camille once more. "Are you two just returning from a lunch meeting?"

Maxwell shook his head. "Camille and I are involved."

Kendra sent him a sharp glare. "If you're expecting me to break down, it's not going to happen. We've been down this road before and we have always gotten back together. This is no different."

She turned to Camille. "Don't fall too deeply for Maxwell because he is going to come back to me."

Dudley signaled for her to join him.

Kendra smiled, then said, "Smooches, lover."

Maxwell took Camille by the hand. "Please don't let her get to you."

"I won't," she responded quietly.

He noted that Camille wasn't in a very talkative mood as they took the elevator to the second floor. Maxwell followed her into her office.

"Sweetheart, are you okay?" he inquired.

"I'm fine," she replied. "I'm just trying to resist the urge to kick Kendra out of this hospital."

Maxwell laughed.

"I don't see how you've been able to put up with her for all of these years." Camille glanced over at him. "I'm sorry. I really shouldn't have said that."

Maxwell shrugged. "It's something I've told myself over and over again."

The night of the Hopewell General charity ball had finally arrived.

The annual event was attended by politicians, prominent businesspeople and anybody on the Alexandria social register.

Maxwell picked up Camille in a stretch limo.

"You look gorgeous," Maxwell complimented as his eyes traveled from her head to her feet, looking her over seductively.

"Mr. Wade, I must say that you look very handsome tonight."

His gaze fell to the smooth expanse of her neck. "That necklace must have set you back a pretty penny."

Camille grinned. "Actually, I have this very generous boyfriend and he thought it went with perfectly with this particular gown."

"That's some gift," Maxwell commented with a smile. "He must love you a whole lot."

Looping her arm through his, Camille responded, "He does."

Twenty minutes later, they made their grand entrance into the Emerald Ballroom at the Ritz-Carlton.

Camille could hardly contain her excitement. She and her staff had worked hard to make the event a success. Everything looked beautiful.

Her eyes bounced around, making sure that everything was in place and nothing had been overlooked.

Camille's lips turned upward when she spotted several of the board members having a conversation. "I'd better go over and say hello," she told Maxwell.

"Okay. I'll be over here sitting all by myself."

Camille gave a short laugh. "Maxwell, I have a feeling you won't be alone for much longer. Don't believe for one minute that I haven't noticed all of the women here watching you. You'd better be glad I'm not really the jealous type."

"Oh, so now you're going to pawn me off on someone else?" he teased. "I'm heartbroken."

"It won't be for long," Camille promised. "I just want to make sure that I haven't missed anything important. This night really has to be perfect. We need to keep the hospital running."

He gazed at her lovingly. "I understand."

Camille checked in with her assistant, and together they walked over to the board members to say hello.

A few minutes later, Camille stole a peek at Maxwell. He was in what looked to be a deep conversation with Thomas and Lia. She smiled and waved when he glanced in her direction.

"I can tell that he really makes you happy," her assistant whispered.

"He does," Camille confirmed.

As Dr. Dudley and his wife entered the ballroom, she went to greet them. She still felt a little uneasy where he was concerned, but Dudley hadn't approached her outside of business.

When she had a free moment, Camille joined Maxwell at the table.

"Did you miss me?" she asked him.

He gave her hand a gentle squeeze. "I did."

She settled back in her chair. "I can relax for a moment. Everything seems to be going well and we're on schedule."

"What would you like to drink?" he asked her.

"Nothing right now," she responded. "Thanks, baby."

Maxwell gave her a look of concern.

Camille was touched to see how much he cared about her well-being. She stroked his cheek. "Don't look so worried. I'm fine."

"When was the last time you ate something?"

Camille considered his question. "Hmm…I guess it was breakfast. I worked through lunch." It had been a crazy day for her, trying to tie up all of the last-minute details for the event.

Maxwell stood up and said, "C'mon."

He led her by the hand over to the buffet table.

Camille struck up a conversation with the woman

in front of her. When she turned to Maxwell, she discovered his attention was elsewhere. She followed his gaze.

"I can't believe her," Maxwell uttered.

"Isn't that Kendra?"

He nodded. "I can't believe she has the camera crew here. But then again, it might turn out to be a good thing. The charity ball will get worldwide exposure."

"I'm sure Dr. Dudley is behind her being here," Camille said. She was not pleased with this turn of events. The chief never once mentioned that Kendra would be in attendance. She was sure that he'd done this on purpose. It was his way of getting back at her and Maxwell.

Camille considered walking over to his table and confronting him, but she would not give Dudley the satisfaction of knowing that he had accomplished his mission.

"This is probably Dudley's way of getting back at me for threatening to go to the board and his wife if he didn't stop harassing his employees," Maxwell stated.

Camille's eyes grew wide in her surprise. "You never told me what transpired between the two of you. I didn't know you blackmailed him."

"I wouldn't call it blackmail. I simply gave him a choice to do the right thing for the good of the hospital."

Camille stole a peek at the tall, leggy supermodel. Kendra looked stunning in the curve-hugging gown she was wearing. The turquoise, strapless beaded dress framed her body perfectly.

Maxwell had surprised Camille with a gorgeous emerald-green gown for the ball, not to mention the diamond necklace. The gown was the same one she'd seen while they were shopping in New York, but would've cost her at least three or four months' salary. The dress had needed no alterations and was a perfect fit.

"Did I tell you how beautiful you look tonight?" he asked her.

Camille looked up at him, smiling. "You did, but I never tire of hearing it." Maxwell had a way of making her feel like she was the most beautiful woman in the world. He made her feel as if she was the only one who mattered. She could understand why Kendra had such a hard time letting go.

She reached up to straighten Maxwell's emerald-green bowtie. "Honey, are you okay?"

"Yeah," he muttered. "I just wish Kendra hadn't decided to crash the ball."

"She's here," Camille stated. "Don't let her ruin the evening for you. I know I'm not. Let Dr. Dudley and the board members keep her entertained." She was a celebrity and they were fawning over her, much to Camille's disappointment. She had worked extremely hard on the fundraiser and didn't want Kendra's appearance to upstage the real reason for the event.

"I suppose I should be grateful," she told Maxwell. "Kendra made a generous donation to the hospital."

"That's good. I'm glad to hear it."

Kendra suddenly appeared out of nowhere, ripping them both out of their good moods.

"Maxwell, I've been looking for you, darling. The photographer wants to take some pictures of us for the newspaper."

Camille kept her expression blank and her temper in check. She glanced across the room and saw Jerome. He gave her a thumbs-up, which she assumed was for her choice in gowns. She hadn't had a chance to tell him that Maxwell deserved all of the credit.

She could feel Maxwell's eyes on her so she looked up, meeting his gaze. "Go ahead. I'll be right here when you get back."

She silently fumed as she watched Kendra practically drape her body over Maxwell's. They took several photographs.

Jerome walked up to her and whistled. "Girl, you look good."

"Thank you." Camille's eyes traveled over to where Maxwell and Kendra were standing. They were talking to a congressman and the president of a major bank.

He followed her gaze. "She's a trip, isn't she?"

"Jerome, you have no idea," Camille muttered, trying to control her anger. "There are not many people that I dislike, but I have to tell you I really don't like her at all."

"Let's get something to drink," Jerome suggested.

Camille nodded. "So who did you bring with you tonight?"

"Julie. We're still kicking it."

"Where is she?" Camille asked, looking around the room.

"Her cousin is here, too. They are probably somewhere running their mouths. Don't worry, she'll find me."

Camille slowly made her way over to where Maxwell and Kendra were talking to the congressman and bank president. She heard the murmur of whispers and swallowed hard. Kendra was deliberately trying to humiliate her in front of her coworkers.

As she posed with Maxwell, Kendra ran her fingers through her long spiral curls.

Camille's cell phone rang so she walked away to take the call, leaving Maxwell in Kendra's clutches for the moment. However, she didn't intend to be gone long. She would be back for her man.

Chapter 18

"What's going on with you?" Maxwell demanded. "Why are you acting like this? Kendra, you know that we're no longer a couple."

"So you say," she shot back. "I'm tired of this charade. You're just using that girl to make me jealous. Well, it worked, baby. *I'm jealous.* I love you and I'll do whatever it takes to get you back, Maxwell."

He shook his head. "I'm not going to let you ruin this evening for Camille."

Kendra glared at him. "I don't care about her."

"Well, I do."

"You only think that you do," she argued. "I'm the only woman you have ever loved. I'm in your blood, Maxwell."

"Kendra, you couldn't be more wrong," he stated before walking away.

It would do no good to debate the issue with her.

They were already drawing enough attention. He meant what he said about not embarrassing Camille. She had worked so hard on this event and he wanted everything to be perfect for her.

Camille couldn't believe Kendra's nerve, but she vowed not to let the woman get to her. After all, Maxwell was committed to her—not the supermodel.

Kendra sauntered up to her, a fake smile on her face. "You put together a very nice party."

She itched to wipe the smug look off the model's face. Camille took a deep breath and adjusted her smile.

"Thanks so much for coming out and supporting Hopewell General," Camille said with feigned sweetness. "Oh…make sure you stay for the auction. We have a fabulous collection of items to bid on. There's something for everyone, including you."

"That must mean that Maxwell's up for auction." Kendra held up the small evening bag she carried. "I'm glad I brought my credit card and checkbook. He's worth every penny."

Camille was grateful when Dr. Dudley intervened and hastily escorted Kendra away.

Maxwell rose to his feet when she walked over to their table. "Is everything okay? I saw you over there with Kendra. It looked a bit intense between you two."

"Everything is fine."

Deep down, it really wasn't fine. Members of the hospital staff were watching her and whispering. As much as Camille tried not to let it bother her, it did. She could feel their eyes watching her every move. More gossip for the hospital grapevine.

Camille posed for some press photos with a couple of U.S. congressmen, a senator and several other VIPs.

She made the rounds smiling and laughing as if she didn't have a care in the world.

Maxwell was careful to keep Kendra away from her, which Camille appreciated. She just wanted to get the night over with. The evening was going well, despite Kendra's presence, however.

When it was time for her to speak, Camille made her way up to the podium with Maxwell's assistance.

"Through the generosity of our donors," she began, "we far exceeded our target and raised more than five million dollars in operating support for the new Bancroft Cancer Treatment Center, named in honor of Richard and Miriam Bancroft.

"Richard Bancroft and his wife were not only financial contributors, they also gave us their time, valuable counsel and personal energy in guiding us toward our goal of creating a treatment center of true distinction. The Bancrofts' endowment of four million dollars joined other generous contributions to make this year a banner year for the hospital's fundraising efforts."

Applause thundered throughout the ballroom.

Camille smiled and waited until the clapping ceased.

"Wow, that was some gift from the Bancrofts," Maxwell commented when she returned to the table.

"The Bancrofts lost their only daughter to cancer when she was only sixteen years old. They said they couldn't honor her life without doing something to help others. Miriam volunteers at the hospital and I see her often visiting or talking to our cancer patients."

Kendra walked over to where they were standing, followed by her camera crew. "Maxwell, darling, I've been looking all over for you. I'd like to add an interview piece for my show."

Camille noted his expression. She could tell that

he was irritated, although he hid his feelings behind a smile.

Kendra gave her a quick once-over before commenting, "This is the coordinator of this fabulous event." She glanced back at her cameraman, and then over at Maxwell before saying, "When Maxwell and I decide to get married, I'm going to give her a call to plan our wedding."

Camille's heart felt as if it were going to crack, but she kept her expression blank.

Finding her voice, she said, "If you two will excuse me, I need to make my rounds."

She walked away as quickly as she could.

Jerome caught up with her. "Hey, what's wrong?"

"Kendra just said on camera that she wanted me to plan her wedding to Maxwell."

"She was messing with you, Camille," Jerome to her. "She knows that she's lost the man and she's trying to make sure you don't get him."

"I'm really not in the mood to deal with her."

"You don't have to deal with the drama. Let Maxwell handle her. If he can't, then maybe he's not the man for you."

Camille nodded in agreement. "I hear you, Jerome. It's just that I…I love him, but I'm not willing to deal with drama from his ex."

Jerome embraced her. "It's going to work out."

She nodded and smiled. "I see someone I need to talk to, so I'll talk to you later. Don't forget to save me a dance."

"I'll try," he teased. "My skills are in high demand tonight."

She and Jerome walked in different directions.

Camille was on her way to speak to her assistant, but halted when Kendra blocked her path.

"Karen," Kendra began. "We need to talk."

"My name is Camille."

She giggled. "Oh, sorry. Anyway, do you have a minute?"

"Not really," Camille responded. "As you've mentioned earlier, I am working."

"Well, I thought maybe we could talk about Maxwell."

Folding her arms across her chest, Camille responded, "Kendra, I don't see any reason why we need to have a discussion about him. I'm pretty sure he's already told you how he feels. There's nothing left to be said—especially between you and me."

"I disagree," Kendra stated. "We can have this discussion in front of everyone or we can do it somewhere private. I really don't care which."

Furious, Camille followed her out of the ballroom.

They stepped inside the empty room next door.

"Look, Kendra, I don't know what you want to talk about, but I don't appreciate your interfering with my job."

Kendra shrugged off her words. "It seems that we're both in love with Maxwell, and for me that presents a huge problem."

"I won't apologize for my feelings," Camille said. "I don't know why I came out here with you because I won't discuss this with you any further. You and Maxwell are not together anymore. Maybe it's time for you to consider moving on. You can't make him love you or want to be with you."

Through clenched teeth, Kendra said, "He is still in love with me. Maybe you're the delusional one here.

Maxwell and I have a long history together. That will never change."

Camille didn't respond.

"What's going on in here?" Maxwell asked, looking from one woman to the other.

"I was just having a little conversation with your friend here," Kendra announced. "I really don't think it's fair what you're doing to her. You shouldn't play games with people's emotions, Maxwell."

Frowning, he uttered, "Excuse me? Kendra, what have you been telling her?"

"The truth." Kendra ran her manicured fingers through her hair. "Baby, I felt that she should know that you still have feelings for me. We always end up back together."

Camille didn't want to hear another word. "I'm not dealing with this," she told them both. "Stay away from me, Kendra."

Maxwell opened his mouth to speak, but she held up her hands. "Right now, I want both of you to stay away from me."

"Sweetheart…" Maxwell began.

Camille walked briskly across the room and through the double doors. She fought back tears as she sought Jerome out.

"Can we take a walk somewhere?" she asked him.

Jerome took one look at her face and nodded. "C'mon."

They walked outside.

"Thanks," Camille murmured. "I just needed to get out of there for a little while."

"What happened between you and Kendra? I saw you two leave the room."

"She felt the need to talk to me about Maxwell,"

Camille said. "She wanted me to know that they always end up back together. She even said I was delusional where Maxwell is concerned. He showed up right after that."

"What did Maxwell say?" Jerome inquired.

"I didn't really give him a chance to say anything," Camille confessed. "I just wanted to be as far away from them as possible. You know how much I hate drama."

"Maxwell really needs to get that ex-girlfriend of his in check," Jerome muttered.

Camille couldn't agree more. "She is so arrogant."

A few minutes later, after Camille calmed down, they walked back inside.

"I have enough to deal with tonight…" Camille's voice died as she laid eyes on Terrence Matthews.

"I never expected to see him here," Jerome said.

He must have seen Terrence at the same moment she did. "I have to hand it to him—Terrence knows how to make an entrance."

Camille saw Thomas and Dr. Dudley walking toward Terrence and said, "I guess I'd better go over there to diffuse the situation."

Camille reached Terrence first. She embraced him. "Hey, you."

He smiled at her. "Hello, beautiful."

"What are you doing here?" she asked in a low voice.

Camille silently noted that Dr. Dudley stopped a few yards away from them. He gestured for Thomas to stop as well. She was relieved that they had decided not to approach Terrence.

"I wanted to come and support you. Despite all that's happened I hope that we can still be friends."

"We *are* friends, Terrence," Camille assured him.

His eyes traveled the room. "You may be the only one who still considers me a friend."

"Terrence, I'm sure that's not true."

His expression showed that he clearly did not believe her. "I'm not going to stay, but I wanted to come see you. I'm sorry it had to come to this, but the hospital didn't treat me very well."

"Terrence, I would hope that if you were in trouble, you'd do whatever was necessary to get better. You are a gifted physician and I'd hate to see you give up medicine or worse, lose the right to practice."

He was quiet for a moment.

She placed a hand to his cheek. "I care about you, Terrence. Believe it or not, we all care about you."

He gestured toward the exit doors. "I should get going. I'm meeting some friends not too far from here. It was good seeing you, Camille. Merry Christmas."

"Same to you, Terrence," she responded.

She watched him leave, relieved that there was not a scene. Camille stole a peek at Maxwell and spotted him walking in her direction. She walked out of the ballroom.

I shouldn't be angry with Maxwell, she kept telling herself. But the truth of it was that she was. Camille hated that Kendra was there, trying to sabotage her event and steal the man she loved.

When she walked into the ladies' room, Camille found Kendra inside. She quickly turned to leave, but paused when she heard her name called.

Turning around, she said, "Kendra, I've already told you that we have nothing to talk about."

"I just wanted to show you my Christmas present from Maxwell." Grinning, Kendra held up her left hand to show off the huge pear-shaped diamond engagement ring. "I want you to know that I was serious about having you plan our wedding."

Kendra's words were like a knife to Camille's heart. She leaned against the door for support. She had no idea how, but she managed to keep her composure. "I don't believe you, Kendra. Why don't you just give it up?"

"Oh honey, I feel so sorry for you," Kendra said. "Maxwell knows that I am the only woman he has ever loved. Sure, we've had our ups and downs, but that's what relationships are all about, don't you think?

"He's tired of the games, too. Maxwell proposed and I accepted." Kendra admired the ring on her finger while Camille struggled to keep her heart from breaking into a million pieces.

"I'm sorry you had to find out like this, but I felt you needed to know the truth."

"No, you're not," Camille countered. "You couldn't wait to tell me your news." She blinked back tears.

Kendra eyed her. "You needed to know that you have no future with Maxwell. He was only using you to make me jealous."

"Go to hell!" Camille shouted. She turned and rushed out of the bathroom. In her haste, she ran straight into Maxwell's path.

"I've been looking for you," he said. "Honey, we need to talk. There's something I need to tell you."

Camille fought back tears. "I don't have time for this right now, Maxwell."

He scanned her face. "You're upset. What's wrong?"

"Maxwell, I'm working. As for whatever you want to talk about—don't bother. I know all I need to know," Camille snapped. "Now leave me alone so that I can focus on my job."

Her eyes searched the room, looking for Jerome. She

really needed her best friend right now, but he was nowhere to be found.

Camille paused to talk to a few dignitaries. Just as she was about to check in with her assistant, Maxwell blocked her path.

"I don't know what's going on right now, but please talk to me, sweetheart. I'll try and fix whatever is wrong."

"There isn't anything to fix," she responded. "Maxwell, I really can't do this right now."

"All right then, but Camille, I'm not going anywhere. I'll be here until you get off."

"I'm surprised," she said. "I figured you and Kendra would be off celebrating. She already shared your news, Maxwell. In fact, she could hardly wait."

Maxwell looked perplexed.

Her assistant walked over to them and interrupted by saying, "Camille, the Bancrofts are leaving, but they wanted to have a word with you."

"I have to go," she said in a low voice. "Maxwell, do me a favor and just leave. What we had is over. That is what you wanted to talk to me about, right?"

Maxwell had never seen this side of Camille before. He had no idea why she was so upset. Was she still angry over the conversation she had with Kendra earlier? Even though she had made it clear that she didn't want to talk to him, Maxwell decided to hang around and wait for her. They definitely needed to talk.

He spotted Kendra and was on his way to find out what she'd told Camille, but then changed his mind. It was better to hear it from Camille, Maxwell decided. He wanted the truth.

"Are you and Camille okay?" Thomas asked,

dropping down in the empty chair beside Matthew. "She looks upset about something."

"Kendra got under her skin, I think," Maxwell responded. "I'm going to talk to her later tonight. I'm not going to let Kendra come between us."

They talked for a few minutes more, and then his best friend left to join his wife at their table.

Camille walked by and Maxwell reached out to grab her hand.

She glared at him. "I'm working."

"I know," he said. "I also know that something's not right. Camille, I hate seeing you like this."

"Then maybe you should leave," Camille suggested.

"We came here together and I'm not leaving you," Maxwell told her.

"I can take a taxi home."

"I'm not going anywhere."

She shrugged.

Something else must have transpired between Camille and Kendra because she was not only angry; she looked heartbroken. Maxwell spotted Kendra standing near the bar and got up to join her. "Did you say something to Camille?" he asked.

She wore a look of confusion. "I don't think so. Why?"

"She's very upset over something and I'm pretty sure that you have something to do with it."

"What did she tell you?" Kendra asked.

"Nothing much," Maxwell responded. "Except that she wants to end our relationship."

"It's for the best," Kendra said. "Honey, why don't we go back to your suite and get reacquainted? I've sent the camera crew to their hotel so it will just be me and you."

Maxwell shook his head. "Kendra, it's not going to happen. How many times do I have to remind you that we are over? Even if Camille doesn't want to be with me, you and I are still over."

"Baby, you can't mean that," she argued. "We've been on and off for the past eight years. *This is what we do*."

"Not this time," he muttered. "I'm going to find Camille."

Kendra followed Maxwell outside of the ballroom.

"I am in love with someone else," he said quietly.

Unshed tears glistened in Kendra's eyes. "She doesn't know what to do with a man like you, Maxwell."

"Contrary to what you'd like to believe, Kendra, she and I are perfect for each other."

"If you want to run down a one-way street, I can't stop you, but don't expect me to come rescue you, Maxwell."

"Understood," he responded.

Kendra gave him one last pleading look before walking away.

All Maxwell could think about was Camille. He vowed to do whatever possible to keep from losing her. Tonight was supposed to perfect. It was supposed to be special.

Maxwell patted the tiny velvet box in his jacket pocket.

Camille was the only woman for him, and he would prove it to her.

Chapter 19

Camille swallowed hard, fighting back tears. Throwing a tantrum wouldn't help her now. She just needed to find someplace private so that she could compose herself.

How could Maxwell do something like this to her? The thought had occurred to her that Kendra could be lying about the engagement, but where did the ring come from? She certainly didn't have it on her finger earlier.

Nothing was making sense to her.

Maxwell had constantly declared his love for her and she had believed him. Now Camille didn't know what to think or whom to trust. In past situations like this she would take a step backward from all parties concerned, in order to decipher the truth.

She spotted Maxwell coming her way. Camille spun on her heel and headed away from him. She wasn't ready to confront him yet.

She was afraid that if she talked to Maxwell now she would fall apart and she didn't want to give him the pleasure of seeing that happen.

"Camille," Maxwell called after her.

She turned around, saying, "Go back to your fiancée."

Her words shocked him. "What fiancée? I'm not engaged."

She swiped at a tear falling from her eye. "Kendra showed me the ring you gave her."

Maxwell's soft brown eyes clung to hers, studying her face. "Honey, I have no idea what you're talking about. I haven't given Kendra anything lately, and definitely not a ring."

Folding her arms across her chest, she questioned, "You're telling me that you never asked her to marry you?"

Maxwell shook his head, thoroughly confused. "Camille, if I intended to marry Kendra I wouldn't have gotten involved with you. I wouldn't play with another person's feelings. Whatever Kendra told you is a lie. We ended things months ago. I did consider her a friend until now."

A shadow of annoyance crossed Camille's face. "Maybe you two are used to playing these types of games, Maxwell, but this is way too much drama for me. Maybe you didn't propose to her, but it doesn't matter. I think it would be better if you'd leave me alone."

He was momentarily speechless in his surprise. Maxwell never expected to hear those words coming from Camille's lips. He was completely baffled and didn't know what to make of this new turn of events.

Recovering from the shock of her words, Maxwell

said, "I'm sorry, but I can't do that. You're the only woman for me, sweetheart. I can't let you go and I don't believe that you can walk away from me that easily. Not if you love me as much as you say you do."

Camille shook her head in disbelief. "I can't do this, Maxwell. I am not going to try and compete with other women for your affection. I—"

Maxwell cut her off by saying, "Honey, you don't have to compete with anyone."

He pulled out a small velvet box and got down on bended knee.

"What are you doing?" Camille asked.

"I love you and I'm going to prove it," he responded. "Will you marry me, Camille?" Maxwell opened the box to reveal a stunning canary diamond engagement ring.

Looking down into his handsome face, Camille could not speak for a few seconds. She initially thought she was in the middle of a dream, but as his words began to permeate every portion of her mind and soul, Camille flung her arms around his neck. "After everything that's happened tonight, you want to marry me?"

"I want you in my life forever," Maxwell confessed. "I was planning on asking you on Christmas morning, but I think now is the right time."

Camille's eyes filled with tears. "I…I don't know what to s-say…."

"Please say yes," he whispered. "Sweetheart, I have never felt this way about another woman. You own my heart."

She really didn't have to think long or hard. Camille knew that there was only one man for her—Maxwell Wade. "Yes, I'll marry you, Maxwell."

He slipped the ring on her finger before rising to

his full height and wrapping his arms around Camille. "You have made me an incredibly happy man."

"I love you," she whispered.

It was a few minutes before Camille realized that they were not alone. She stepped out of Maxwell's embrace to find Kendra watching them, her TV crew a few yards away.

Maxwell followed her gaze. "How long have you been standing there, Kendra?" he asked.

"Long enough," she responded coolly. Kendra tossed her waist-length curls over her shoulder. "I suppose I should say congratulations or something, but I won't. I've never been a graceful loser and there's no point in starting now."

Maxwell wrapped an arm around Camille, and then said, "I wish you well, Kendra."

She glared at them. "Whatever."

Kendra turned to find her crew recording. "Cut the frigging camera off!" she shouted. "This is my show. I'd better not see one frame showing Maxwell or his little girlfriend of the moment."

They watched her stalk off, spewing out venom.

"I guess my proposal won't make it on national TV," Maxwell said with a short laugh.

Camille peered at the ring on her finger. "I feel like I'm dreaming," she murmured.

"It's no dream, sweetheart. I proposed and you accepted. We have an ironclad agreement to become husband and wife."

She turned to face Maxwell. "I can't wait to start my life with you."

"So does that mean we're having a short engagement?" Maxwell asked, grinning.

"Not exactly," Camille replied. "I need time to plan a wedding."

He feigned disappointment. "Okay, sweetheart, but I don't want to wait too long."

Camille eyed her engagement ring once more, and then said, "I really need to get back to work. The night's not over yet."

Maxwell kissed her. "I love you, Camille."

"I love you, too."

Camille and Maxwell walked hand in hand back into the ballroom, where the charity ball was still in full swing.

"I need to make my rounds," she told him. "But I'll see you in a few minutes."

Jerome rushed to her side. "Okay, spill. Why are you floating in here with a grin that could light up New York?"

"I don't know what you're talking about," Camille said.

"Do not lie to me, girl. I know you." Jerome backed away and openly observed her, his eyes traveling from her face to her left hand. He placed a hand to his chest. "I see Christmas came early for you, Camille."

"Maxwell and I are engaged," she said in a low voice.

Jerome hugged her. "Congratulations. You deserve it." Lowering his voice, he said, "This news is going to upset the females at Hopewell, but don't worry. I'll be there to pick up the slack."

Shaking her head, Camille laughed.

"What's going on?" Isabelle asked when she joined them. "I couldn't help overhearing Jerome congratulate you. What's the big news?"

"Maxwell and I just got engaged."

Isabelle pasted on a smile. "Wow, I wasn't expecting

that. I thought maybe you'd gotten a job promotion or something." She paused a moment before adding, "Congratulations, Camille."

"Thank you, Isabelle, but do me a favor and don't say anything yet. Maxwell and I would like to be the ones to announce that we're getting married."

"Then you may want to take off that rock," Isabelle responded. "You know the hospital grapevine."

Camille didn't remove her ring. They would have preferred making the announcement, but then again, she really didn't care if everyone in the room found out—she was just that happy.

With Kendra gone, Camille was able to fully relax and enjoy the rest of the evening. However, nothing thrilled her more than when the charity ball drew to a close. She and Maxwell were looking forward to a private celebration once they returned to her town house.

"I'm so glad this night is over," Camille murmured as she removed her shoes.

Maxwell sat down beside her on the edge of her bed. "I'll glad to finally have you all to myself."

Playing with the ring on her finger, Camille said, "I told Jerome about our engagement. He's my best friend and I was bursting with happiness. Besides, he noticed the ring on my finger."

"Honey, that's fine." Maxwell removed his shirt.

"Isabelle also knows," she announced. "I asked her not to tell anyone else, but I'm pretty sure by Monday, the entire hospital will know."

"I don't have a problem with it," he said with a shrug. "I want the whole world to know that I have the women of my dreams."

"Kendra told me that you had proposed to her."

"Is that why you were so upset? Why did you believe her?"

"She had on a huge engagement ring. Kendra didn't have it on earlier. What was I supposed to think?"

"We were engaged a couple of years ago," Maxwell said. "That was probably the ring you saw on her finger."

"Oh," Camille said. "I don't know why I believed her in the first place. I should have trusted you."

"She can be very convincing."

"Maxwell, I was wrong for not believing in your love for me. I'm really sorry."

He kissed her. "Honey, I understand. Going forward, I want you to come talk to me before you just assume the worst."

"Hopefully, we won't have another issue like this," Camille said. "Especially since you're going to be my husband."

"Your husband," Maxwell repeated. "I love the sound of that."

"What's going on?" Camille inquired. Maxwell had been on the phone for most of the morning. When he hung up, he told her to get dressed.

"Why all the rush?" she inquired.

"I hired a masseuse," Maxwell explained. "I thought maybe you could use a massage after all the hard work you put in for the fundraiser and the Christmas Eve party this afternoon for the pediatric wing."

Camille gave him a smile. "Honey, thank you for being so thoughtful, especially after the way I treated you last night. I really appreciate it." She was genuinely touched by his thoughtfulness. More importantly, her aching body could use a massage.

"I intend to take care of you for the rest of my life, sweetheart," he told her.

The masseuse arrived.

Maxwell had another surprise in store for Camille later that afternoon. He made a phone call to confirm the details.

After her massage, Camille felt like a new woman.

"I really needed that," she told Maxwell. "You are so sweet to me."

He smiled. "We have to leave for the hospital soon."

"I know," Camille responded. "You're going to the Christmas party?"

Maxwell nodded. "I know it's for the kids, but I thought I could lend a hand with giving out the presents."

"Sure."

He couldn't wait to see her face when she realized what he'd done. Maxwell knew that Camille would be thrilled. It would be a dream come true for her. He wanted to make all of her dreams come to life.

Camille smiled as she watched Maxwell with the children. He had read the Christmas story to them and now they were sitting with him, asking a million questions. He was very patient with them.

She glanced over at the gifts stacked in the corner. "Where did they come from?" she asked her assistant. "Are they more donations?"

"Yes," the assistant responded. "They arrived first thing this morning."

Camille walked over to Maxwell. "Looks like you were having a lot of fun with the children."

"I am," he confirmed. "How about you?"

She nodded.

Maxwell embraced her. "Kendra was right about one thing. You really do know how to throw a nice party."

Camille looked up at him. "If you really want to see a party, just wait until our wedding."

Dr. Dudley strolled in, dressed as Santa Claus. The children were ecstatic.

Billy, the young patient who had rapidly become a favorite of hers, walked over to her and grabbed her hand. "C'mon, freen. Let's see Santa."

Camille glanced over at Maxwell and asked, "Hey, are you coming?"

"I'm going to go talk to Thomas about something," he responded. "I'll join you and Billy in a few minutes."

She smiled and nodded.

The time came for Santa's helpers to pass out Christmas gifts to each of the children. Santa, along with volunteers dressed as elves, had already handed out gifts to the children who were unable to attend the party in their hospital rooms.

Maxwell gave Billy a present that contained a fire truck. The little boy was thrilled.

"This is just want I wanted," he said, his eyes bright with excitement. "I told Santa and he got me one."

Camille smiled. "That's great, Billy."

"We have more gifts for the children and for Hopewell General," Thomas announced. "Maxwell Wade has made a generous donation that enabled us to not only give each child a video game console, but each hospital room in the pediatric wing will now be equipped with one."

Stunned, Camille looked up at Maxwell. "Why didn't you tell me?"

"Honey, I wanted to surprise you. I knew this was a dream of yours and I wanted to make it come true."

"Thank you." Tears of happiness rolled down her face. Camille was only mildly surprised by Maxwell's generosity, but she hadn't expected him to fulfill one of her deepest desires.

Maxwell gently wiped away her tears. "Sweetheart, I didn't mean to make you cry."

"You have no idea how much your gift means to me. Maxwell, look at the children."

His eyes followed hers. He could hear the excitement in the kids' voices and see the happiness on their faces. Despite their illnesses, the children already seemed in better spirits.

"You did something really wonderful," Camille said.

"I can't take credit for this," he responded. "This was your idea."

Maxwell saw Billy struggling to open his box, and went over to assist him. Camille walked around the room, pausing every now and then to talk to the children or help them with their presents or assist them with getting something to eat.

Isabelle walked over to her. "You're really lucky, Camille. What Maxwell just did for these babies is so sweet."

She agreed. "I am very lucky."

When they were back at her town house, Camille took Maxwell by the hand and led him over to the sofa.

They sat down side by side.

"Maxwell, I can't tell you enough how grateful I am to have you in my life. What you've done for Hopewell General…it's incredible and very generous."

"What good is having all of this wealth if I can't do something good with it?" he asked. "I believe that I have been blessed to be a blessing."

"I love you more and more each day because of the man that you are—not because of what you have."

Maxwell took her hand in his. "Camille, I love you so much. What matters to you also matters to me. We're going to make a great team, don't you think?"

Camille smiled. "Yes, I do."

"I hope that you know Kendra is out of my life for good."

She gazed at him lovingly. Camille gave his hand a gentle squeeze. "I trust you, Maxwell. I never should have doubted your love for me."

"Camille, I need you to know that you will always own my heart," Maxwell told her. "I came to Virginia for one case, but I found another. Probably one of the most important cases I will ever encounter."

Camille frowned. "What case are you referring to?"

"You," he responded with a grin. "I have a bad case of desire. Right now, all I can think about is making love to you."

"I think I like the sound of that," she murmured. "But first, I need to pack for our trip."

They were leaving later this evening on the jet. Camille and Maxwell were spending Christmas with her family in Richmond. They would then travel to New York later in the week to spend New Year's with his family.

Camille had almost finished packing when Maxwell walked into her bedroom.

Their eyes met and held.

Without a word, Maxwell pulled Camille into his arms, touching his lips to hers.

Her kisses would last him an eternity, he decided. There would never be another woman who would make him feel the way he did around Camille.

Maxwell had done everything he could to convince Camille to move to New York, but she insisted on staying in Virginia and with the hospital until after their wedding. She had promised Dudley that she would help select and train her replacement. He shouldn't be surprised by her decision—he would have done the same thing. However, in a few months, she would be his wife.

He smiled at the thought of marrying Camille.

What are you smiling about?" she asked him.

"I was thinking about our wedding. I can't wait to make you my wife."

Camille took Maxwell by the hand. "You know this means that you're going to be stuck with me forever?"

He laughed. "I can't think of any other place I'd rather be than by your side."

"Well, I'm all packed," Camille announced, looking over her shoulder at the suitcase on the bed. "I'm looking forward to this Christmas, and every Christmas, in New York."

"It's the first of many more," Maxwell murmured as he pulled her into his arms. "We have a lifetime of memories ahead of us."

* * * * *

REQUEST YOUR FREE BOOKS!

2 FREE NOVELS
PLUS 2 *FREE GIFTS!*

KIMANI™ ROMANCE

Love's ultimate destination!

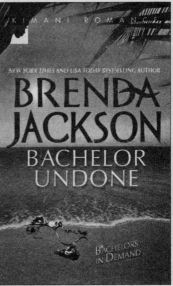